THE COBRA

AND THE KEY

THE COBRA

AND THE KEY

SAM SHELSTAD

BRINDLE
AND GLASS

Brindle & Glass

An imprint of TouchWood Editions

touchwoodeditions.com

Edited by Kate Kennedy

Proofread by Senica Maltese

Cover design by David Drummond

Interior design by Sara Loos

The author thanks Katie Shelstad, Michael LaPointe, Kamil Chajder, Sam Haywood, Megan Philipp, Fawn Parker, Binnie Kirshenbaum, Michael Hingston, Anna Fitzpatrick, Tori Elliott, Curtis Samuel, Kate Kennedy, Senica Maltese, David Drummond, and Sara Loos.

CATALOGUING DATA AVAILABLE FROM LIBRARY AND ARCHIVES CANADA

ISBN 9781990071126 (softcover)

ISBN 9781990071133 (electronic)

TouchWood Editions acknowledges that the land on which we live and work is within the traditional territories of the Lkwungen (Esquimalt and Songhees), Malahat, Pacheedaht, Scia'new, T'Sou-ke and W̱SÁNEĆ (Pauquachin, Tsartlip, Tsawout, Tseycum) peoples.

We acknowledge the financial support of the Government of Canada through the Canada Book Fund and the Canada Council for the Arts, and of the Province of British Columbia through the British Columbia Arts Council and the Book Publishing Tax Credit.

This book was printed using FSC®-certified, acid-free papers, processed chlorine-free, and printed with soya-based inks.

Printed in Canada

27 26 25 24 23   1 2 3 4 5

For Molly

Prologue

Imagine you are standing in a gymnasium with numerous wooden chests spread out across the floor. Each chest contains one of two things: either a cobra, or a story. As much as you do not want to interact with the dangerous snakes, your curiosity is too great. It's human nature to crave stories. We need them. So you gamble and open up one chest. It's a story. You sit down and read, relieved to have avoided an encounter with one of the cobras and grateful that you get to enjoy a story. Once finished, however, you find yourself feeling anxious. The story was fine, but nothing special. You need to open another chest in the hopes of finding another, better story. In fact, you will not be satisfied until all non-snake chests have been opened and you have recovered every possible story. And so, inevitably, you open a cobra chest. You are bitten and the poison slowly kills you.

Let's now go back and add to this scenario a much larger chest, which sits in the centre of the gymnasium and contains an endless supply of stories. These stories, it turns out, are the greatest stories ever told. Beautiful, impactful, masterful stories—much more interesting and satisfying on every level than the ones contained in the smaller chests. The only problem is that this large chest is locked. And the key to open it is located inside the stomach of one of the cobras.

Now, when you go around opening chests, you actually want to open a snake chest. Because if you do, and are able to kill the cobra before it bites you, you might find the key to the big chest. Then you can retrieve the really good stories.

The cobras, you see, represent various problems that writers encounter: problems relating to plot or characterization, for example. The aim of this book is to teach you how to kill the cobras before they can bite and poison you. Once you finish this book, you will no longer fear the cobras. You will be able to kill these different cobras and eventually find the key, open the big chest, and gain access to the higher pedigree of stories.

Now let's get to work.

Getting Started

1

All you need to write is a piece of paper and a pen. Most other forms of artmaking require expensive equipment or intense scheduling. Think of everything that must come together for a symphony to reach its audience: all the musicians and their instruments, the endless rehearsals, booking the concert hall, and so on. Meanwhile, a gifted novelist can simply write "Paul listened to a beautiful song" and achieve the same effect. Or try and comprehend the expenses, time, and coordination that go into a film production. Months or even years of work, involving hundreds of people, and it all costs a fortune. Yet the slobs watching the finished product need to continuously shove popcorn and candies into their mouths in order to enjoy themselves. And then half of them fall asleep in the theatre anyway. The writer wins again. What about paintings? one might suggest. The tools required aren't terribly expensive and a compelling work can be completed in a relatively short period of time. And don't they say a picture is worth a thousand words? With a couple of mouse clicks, however, a writer can copy and paste an image of a painting right into their book. Checkmate.

2

If you're having trouble getting started, a nice way to loosen up is to use writing prompts. Search "writing prompts" online, and you'll find endless examples. Sometimes these exercises can actually lead to completed, published stories—even successful novels.

For instance, one writing prompt I found challenges you to write about a stranger sitting next to you on the train and then leaving behind a mysterious package when they disembark. Do you investigate the package? What's inside? If I were to engage in this exercise, I might have my protagonist open the package and find a balloon with a note stuck to it that says "pop me." Curious, my protagonist searches around in their bag, finds a pen, and proceeds to pop the balloon. What they don't realize is that the stranger was an assassin and the balloon is filled with a poisonous gas. This works well because it's surprising that the balloon has poison in it and it gives me an exciting ending.

Another prompt asks what your character would do if, out for a walk one morning, they come across a hooded figure standing on the other side of the street, pointing at your character and mumbling something. What do they want? Again, I think the balloon of poisonous gas could work well here. The hooded figure is an assassin who hands your character the balloon and tells them to pop it when they get home. After some trepidation and searching around the house for something sharp, they do so, and die from the poison. Another exciting ending. The poison balloon actually works for quite a few of these.

3

Sometimes the title of a book or story will come later in the process, whereas other times it can actually be a starting point. A good, solid title can guide your work from the beginning by establishing subject, tone, and theme. The 1,200-page novel I've been working on for several years and only recently finished composing is titled *The Emerald*. I landed on *The Emerald* early on in the process, and having it there to inspire me in moments of doubt has been a wonderful creative boon. It's the perfect title: *The Emerald*. It's simple, easy to remember, and brilliantly mysterious. What is this emerald? Where did it come from? How big is it and what does it look like, exactly? Is it very expensive? What happens to it? With two words—one, really—I've already grabbed your attention and filled your mind with interesting questions.

4

If you're having trouble coming up with a title for your work, walk over to the bookshelf and peruse the spines. What titles work for you, and what ones fall flat? Looking over at my own shelf, I see *The Brothers Karamazov*. A fantastic title—what a crazy name, "Karamazov," which makes me imagine these insane brothers. I spot *Infinite Jest*, which suggests that the book will have no conflict and is therefore unsuccessful as a title. Better luck next time. Now I see *Bear* by Marian Engel. How could I not read this immediately? A bear is conflict incarnate. Success. Then I come to *Slaughterhouse Five*, which is a curious example. The word "slaughterhouse" is quite good, but "five" makes me think I have the wrong book: surely, I need to start with the first in the series, *Slaughterhouse*. Too confusing. Finally, my eyes fall on Flannery O'Connor's *The Violent Bear It Away*. I'm definitely getting Marian Engel vibes here. But while the first three words would make for an incredible title, this is spoiled by the inclusion of the last two words. I would have swapped out "It Away" for "Runs Amok."

5

Grammar is important and if you find this an area in which you could use some help, I recommend the concise and widely praised *The Elements of Style* by Strunk and White. Learning and remembering all of the finicky little grammar rules can be rather challenging, however. Luckily, there is a workaround: if your narrator is an idiot, then they wouldn't use proper grammar. Write about dumb people, have them narrate your stories, and you needn't worry over grammar again.

6

The life of the artist is one of passion and intensity, but there is a trade-off. While my ex-lover Molly may initially have been drawn to me because of my intriguing occupation, she was not prepared for the sometimes taxing job of being partnered with a novelist. After nearly a year of dating, she only recently left me. I'm heartbroken, yes, but I also see her position. It can be difficult to understand the artistic temperament. When she would suggest we go out somewhere for dinner, or to socialize with other couples, I would regularly have to turn her down. I'm busy, I'd say, can't you see? There's always so much work to do when you're trying to create a masterpiece, and there often isn't time for dates. I had to skip out on meeting her friends, her sisters. She grew accustomed to my last-minute cancellations. And then there was the time Molly slipped on some ice and I failed to visit her in the hospital. I was in the middle of important revisions at the time, though. It's tough for regular people to understand this, but sometimes the work must absolutely come first.

On the other hand, there are incredible benefits to dating a writer. How exciting it must be that this person you're with makes their living creating worlds. Like a god. Here I am, these significant others must think, wondering what to eat for dinner like a simpleton, while the mind of the person I'm holding hands with is a million miles away, contemplating complex societies of people they invented, with all these characters gracefully interacting and creating moments of pure gravitas. While there are some minor drawbacks, it's actually quite an honour to be dating a writer. It might be helpful to remind your romantic partners of this fact.

7

The life of a writer is not always glamorous. There are certain hard truths about the writing life you'll need to come to terms with, if this is something you wish to pursue in earnest. There's not a lot of money to be made in writing fiction. Sure, Stephen King might sleep atop a mountain of cash. The *Life is Pie* guy probably drives a nice car. But most of us do not earn enough from book sales to pay the bills, and thus we have to supplement our incomes with side jobs. Often this takes the form of teaching creative writing, or moonlighting as a copywriter. In my case, I work as a cashier at Value Village, a thrift department store. The thing is, I don't mind doing so because the whole experience is actually research into human behaviour. My side job feeds into my true occupation. A lot of my co-workers live depressing lives and come into work with these sad sack attitudes, but I hold my head high. They work at Value Village, and I "work" there. While I definitely am standing there, physically ringing through customer purchases and calling for a supervisor when someone wants to return a bag of wet clothing, I'm also suspended above the scene, detached, studying everything, making interesting observations. Also, I've taken on the mission of personally curating the books section of the store. While not actually part of my job description, I sneak over to the books whenever I can and perform the public service of making sure the important literature is front and centre. Dull, overhyped novels get sent to the bottom shelf—the spines facing inwards. Sometimes I'll even sneak particularly offensive volumes into the trash. My efforts go largely unappreciated by the tired-looking customers who pick through the shelves like sickly rodents, but I press on in the hopes that even one Modern Library edition of *To the Lighthouse* makes it into the arms of the elusive "real reader."

8

Routine is of great importance. If you're going to take the writing life seriously, you need to write every day. It doesn't matter if the sun is shining and your best friend is hosting a barbeque. It doesn't matter if your little tummy is upset and you just want to lie down. It doesn't matter if your girlfriend has slipped on some ice and is stuck alone in a hospital room, awaiting surgery. You are a writer, and you must write. A common misconception about writing, however, is that the writer must always be typing to be engaged in the act of writing. This is simply not true. I could be pacing the room, combing my brain for the next bit of dialogue. Or perhaps I'm in the park, strolling by the duck pond, untangling character motivations and coming up with interesting chapter transitions. In fact, a writer can write without even thinking about their work. I can be watching TV, giving the show my undivided attention, and still be writing. That's because a focused, experienced writer has trained their subconscious to constantly be working on stories, even if their conscious mind is fixated on something entirely unrelated. A lot of the time, when I'm writing, it might look like I'm not doing anything at all.

9

A note on writer's block: it is a real phenomenon, and you will likely encounter it at some point. After weeks or months of productive writing, all of a sudden you hit a wall. You can't figure out what should happen next in your story. You are a writer, and you are blocked. When this happens, insert a new, unhinged character into the story and have them go on a shooting rampage. Then your other characters will have to deal with that whole mess, and you've bought yourself a few more chapters of content.

10

You will often hear writers bandy about the adage "write what you know." By mining your own life for artistic material, you'll be coming at your work from a unique perspective that no other writer can share. You might think if you're spending all of your time sitting at a desk, trying to come up with unique stories, what is there to write about? How many stories about depressed novelists do we need? But the point is not to only write about your own day-to-day existence, but to look at the people around you and borrow from their experiences. For example, due to the rising cost of rent in Toronto, where I live, I recently had to move in with my uncle Herman. He provides a torrent of material for my work. My uncle Herman is mentally ill and believes that the police are trying to kill him with electronic pulses, which is why he dismantled our smoke alarm and carbon monoxide detector. He is certain that our building super is sacrificing foster children in the boiler room and leaving cryptic clues pointing to this in all posted notices. Although living with my uncle can be difficult—he often interrupts my writing by tackling me to the ground, insisting that I'm messaging the police chief about his activities—he provides me with an endless supply of material for my funny sidekick characters. If you don't have a psychologically unbalanced person in your life to draw amusing ideas from, make it a priority to find one.

11

Drawing inspiration from your life can actually help you work through trauma. I've mentioned that I was recently broken up with by my ex-lover Molly, and that this development has caused me incredible stress. While I do feel that this separation is temporary, and will only bring us closer together in the long run, the feeling of rejection is still painful. I've decided to work through this pain by writing a novel based on my relationship (thus far) with Molly. Our story is actually quite interesting: Molly is significantly older than me and, in fact, a friend of my mother's, which meant we initially had to spend a great deal of effort keeping our companionship a secret. Further, even though Molly's previous relationship was basically non-existent in any practical sense by the time we met, she was technically married to another man. Revisiting and re-evaluating all of this drama from the comfort of my writing desk has been an effective way to temper my heartache and sort through my feelings. Since I'm simultaneously working on this Molly novel as well as the writing guide you are currently reading, I will periodically refer to my progress on the Molly novel throughout the guide, to give you greater insight into my creative process. And who knows, by the time you are reading this writing guide, perhaps my Molly novel will have been completed and published to critical acclaim. Maybe the success of the Molly novel is what drew you to my writing guide, in fact. Maybe *The Emerald* came out with a small press, won several awards, and caught the attention of various literary agents and editors from large publishing houses, which meant that a bidding war erupted over the rights to my Molly novel. Wouldn't it be interesting to get a behind-the-scenes look at the creation of an international bestseller and critical darling, written from the perspective of someone who, at the time of composing this guide, is yet to be discovered as an important literary talent? No matter what level of acclaim my work receives in the future, I only hope that I'm able to aid others along the way. Perhaps I should be spending less time trying to support emerging writers and more time trying to further my own career, but I feel called to help those who are starting out. I guess that's just the way I am.

12

The thing with writing a novel is that it takes quite a bit of time, whereas a short story can be completed in a relatively short period. Of course, a short story might take quite a bit of time itself. And a novel could potentially end up being written quickly. Generally, however, a novel will take more time and a short story will be written rather quickly. But not always.

13

What should you have on your writer's desk? Whether you write with pen and paper or on a computer, you obviously will need your preferred composition tool. A beverage is advised, so you don't become dehydrated during the long hours of creative work. I always start my writing day with a can of Sprite within reach. Certainly, the writing guide you're reading now will be an invaluable resource to keep on hand. Something to spark your creativity or draw inspiration from can also be helpful: if you're writing a story based on your childhood experience playing in Little League, pull your old baseball mitt out from storage and set it on your desk. If your novel takes place in the trenches of World War II, place a few soldier figurines nearby to encourage you. Since I'm writing something based on my relationship with Molly, I have a framed photo of my ex-lover propped up next to my computer. I snapped the picture myself, the first time she came over to my apartment. That day, my mom came to take Uncle Herman out for lunch and I had the place to myself, for once. Molly was standing in my kitchen and the dim light softened her features—I knew I had to capture the moment. Then I made her a sandwich and we had sex in my bed. It's really a nice picture. I could easily have a career as a successful photographer if I wanted to. And Molly looks stunning in the green blouse I bought her for her seventieth. Actually, Molly bought the blouse. I was busy with my *The Emerald* submission at the time and had to cancel our birthday plans, so I told Molly to pick out a nice gift for herself and I'd reimburse her later. She ended up buying the green blouse, which suited her perfectly, but then I felt weird just giving her money. Even Molly agreed that it would have been strange. A funny little story, which might make its way into the novel, in fact. But anyway, it's useful to have Molly there, because looking at her helps me remember details from our time together. I think I'd keep the photo beside my computer regardless of its relevance to my writing project, however. Molly is just so pretty and has such a pretty smile, and she's so talented at using makeup to hide her age. She looks like someone in her early forties, which is much closer to my generation (born in the eighties, so technically I'm a millennial). And the photo is a reminder that we'll be back together soon and everything will be okay. "Keep writing," Molly says with her eyes, "and before you know it, I'll be back in your arms. Be patient, Sam. I miss you, and I can't wait to have sex with you in your bed." If you're going to be spending a great deal of time sitting at your desk, writing, it's important to have some kind of special object nearby to keep you motivated. What is *your* photograph of Molly?

14

While I'm mostly interested in literary fiction, genre experiments can be quite interesting to play around with. One of the most popular—and profitable—genres is the thriller. While I haven't written a thriller myself, I easily could, and I'm certain it would be an instant success. The trick with these stories is to include a large cast of sketchy and suspicious characters. Pretty much everyone in the book should be a likely suspect in the novel's central crime. They should all say mean things and have a history of criminal activity and no alibi. One character, however, should be incredibly kind and sweet. They should be cartoonishly small. Include a scene where they ask for help opening a jar. Show them hugging a dog. Your reader will never suspect that they are behind the crime, but at the end of the novel, you reveal that this nice character did the murder.

15

Science fiction is lowbrow entertainment and an insult to literature. Do not engage with sci-fi on any level. There was a kid at my middle school who used to call me "the ugly boy" and regularly threw my backpack on the school roof. That same kid is now a published sci-fi author, which should give you an idea of the kind of people involved in that whole scene. Consider this passage from Frank Herbert's *Dune*, widely considered a high water mark for the genre:

> Thufir Hawat, his father's Master of Assassins, had explained it: their mortal enemies, the Harkonnens, had been on Arrakis eighty years, holding the planet in quasi-fief under a CHOAM Company contract to mine the geriatric spice, melange. Now the Harkonnens were leaving to be replaced by the House of Atreides in fief-complete—an apparent victory for the Duke Leto. Yet, Hawat had said, this appearance contained the deadliest peril, for the Duke Leto was popular among the Great Houses of the Landsraad.

What a load of horseshit.

16

This might come as a surprise, but I believe it is worthwhile for all writers to familiarize themselves with the romance section of the bookstore. It can give you great insight into the human psyche to see how the written word is used to titillate bored housewives and lonely spinsters. By analyzing the strict formula these books generally adhere to, a writer can peer into the psychosexual underworld of modern life and study the desires of an entire generation of repressed suburbanites. Reading romance fiction, as well as amateur erotic fiction found online, will expand your understanding of the often sexually charged relationship between author and audience. Pornographic videos can also be of service in this regard. A serious novelist should be watching quite a bit of pornography. This includes softcore porn, hardcore porn, amateur, gay, straight, bondage, gang bang, gonzo, alternative pornography, MILF pornography, deepfake porn, celebrity sex tapes, hentai, bukkake, gokkun, animal porn, tentacle erotica, clothed male/naked female, clothed female/naked male, and of course pornography utilizing virtual reality technology.

17

A writer's task never stops—some of your best work can even come while you are asleep. Many celebrated novels and award-winning short stories were inspired by dreams. Get into the habit of keeping a journal beside the bed, so you can jot down your dream experiences upon waking. You never know when some strange scene cooked up by your subconscious might provide you with a new story idea. Last night, for instance, I dreamt that my uncle Herman came into my room in the middle of the night, straddled me on the bed, and wrapped his hands around my throat. I still remember the intense, cold stare on his face, illuminated by the moonlight coming in through my window. Mumbling something about "psychic theft." The dream was so vivid, when I woke up in the morning my neck even felt a little sore. Could this turn into a new piece of flash fiction?

18

Why write? It's not just about getting a good publishing deal. Yes, I recently heard from an editor at Ballast Books, a celebrated San Francisco press known for releasing daring and impactful titles, who said they enjoyed the chapters from *The Emerald* I'd sent them and that they'd be interested in seeing the complete manuscript. This is certainly good news, but that's not *why* I write. Sure, I've come to realize how all the other literary houses and small presses either ignoring or rejecting my *The Emerald* pitch is actually a good thing, because it's the kind of work that needs to come out with the perfect press, which I now believe Ballast Books to be. If some lesser publisher with questionable taste were to take on my novel, they would surely taint the work and kill off its essence. Ballast Books will give *The Emerald* the love and care it requires. And realizing this has been a great vindication, and the respect I have for this editor from Ballast Books—we'll call him Abe—is doubled, because the fact that he can see the immense value in my novel, which flew right over the heads of the other editors, speaks volumes for Abe's character and keen eye for talent. But that's not why I write either.

And though my weekly email check-ins with Abe to see if he's read the manuscript and gauge his enthusiasm have been largely ignored, I know this is only because Abe, though an intelligent acquiring editor, may lack the social skills and business acumen normally required of someone in his position. I just need to keep on him. He'll write me back. I can already picture *The Emerald* with the iconic Ballast Books logo on the spine. They really have some interesting novels and story collections under their belt. It's not just budget travel guides, which it might seem like at first if you visit their website. There's a separate page for the fiction and poetry titles. But that's not why I write. I write because of my passion for storytelling.

Character

19

Every character in your story needs to be memorable. When a character we haven't seen for thirty pages shows up again, the reader ought to recognize them immediately—even if they only had one line of dialogue and then disappeared. One way to make your characters memorable is to give them crazy names. For example, imagine a character who works in an office and wears glasses. He's this white guy and he doesn't really like his job, but he goes in every day. Nothing really stands out about this character so far, right? Well, guess what? The guy I just described is named Dilbert.

All it takes is one interesting trait for a character to stand out on the page. Maybe they have really long arms, so that their hands drag along the ground. Maybe they have a police siren strapped to their head and it's always going off. Maybe they have some sort of strange medical condition where they need to ride around in *two* wheelchairs. By treating every character like a real, breathing human being in this way, your work will feel more alive.

20

The reader will want to know what your protagonist looks like right away. Bringing this up first thing can feel awkward, however; we're only just beginning on our narrative journey and the author is already poking their nose in, making their presence known while they list off facial features and hairstyles. But the reader will become more immediately immersed in the world of the story if they're able to clearly picture your main character in their mind. One clever way to accomplish this is to have a blind person come up and introduce themselves to your protagonist on page one. The blind person can ask your protagonist to describe their physical appearance, since the blind person obviously can't see for themselves, and now you have a more natural way to tell the reader what your main character looks like. Then you can keep this blind person around as a kind of sidekick who constantly prompts your protagonist to provide detailed descriptions of the things they encounter in the story.

21

Try and step outside of your usual social circle every so often, and make an effort to meet the kinds of people you wouldn't normally encounter in your day-to-day life. Personally engaging with the diverse range of humanity the world has to offer will help you create more interesting characters. For instance, when I finished a draft of *The Emerald* last year, I decided to focus test the novel on my mother's book club. I convinced Mother to choose *The Emerald* when it came time for her pick, printed off copies for everyone, and hovered around in the background when the women gathered in Mother's living room to discuss my work. While the focus test itself ended up being entirely unhelpful— these unsophisticated seniors had no sense of literary value—it did expose me to a group of people from a different walk of life. These bored grandmothers see the world differently, and now I can draw on them for my simple-minded, elderly characters. Not only do these women have laughably shallow insights when it comes to art, but they can be tactless and actually cruel in their criticisms. They wouldn't know good writing if it hit them in their wrinkled heads. They only like what Reese Witherspoon tells them to like. But this is helpful information to have, and I can now write about rude, simple, elderly women with confidence. I suspect that the majority of the book club didn't even bother to read my novel, and were just kind of going along with whatever this one woman said. And that one woman, who seemed to be the group's ringleader, was actually the dumbest one of all.

22

Readers need to root for your protagonist. Your main character must be sympathetic or you will lose your audience. This doesn't mean your protagonist cannot act in a cruel manner or have flaws. They can be an anti-hero. If you go down this road, however, you need to pay for their ugly behaviour with sympathetic gestures. The most effective way to accomplish this is to show your protagonist being nice to animals. If your character pets a stranger's dog on the first page, you've bought yourself a nasty, insensitive comment on page two. If they leave out a saucer of milk for a stray cat in the neighbourhood, they can later shoplift from a locally owned business. Nursing an injured bird back to health will buy you adultery. Your protagonist can even commit murder, but you'll need to establish that they run an entire animal sanctuary first. To really sell this, make sure to include details like sickly, malnourished horses and rescued circus monkeys with bandages on their heads.

23

One interesting exercise is to imagine what your character would do for their segment of the *Saturday Night Live* title sequence, where each cast member is depicted enjoying a different aspect of New York City nightlife. Maybe they're ordering from a hot dog cart, or laughing with friends in an Irish pub. They could be skateboarding in Washington Square Park, singing karaoke, or hailing a taxi. What your character would choose in order to succinctly highlight their personality will not only give you an idea of their interests, but it will grant you greater insight into their self-perception: how they see themselves, and how they want the world to see them. As an aside, I always thought that it would be funny, if I were to have a little nightlife scene in the SNL title sequence, to be struggling along a busy Manhattan street in a wheelchair, frowning. Then I look up at the camera with a huge grin, get out of the chair, and start walking normally. That way I'd be guaranteed a laugh every episode, even if my sketches didn't make it to air.

24

Learning about people from different walks of life can help you build characters, but you need to remember that these people are first and foremost individuals. Just because they belong to a certain type or group doesn't mean that their personality should be entirely informed by this belonging. People are complex and often full of contradictions. I characterized my mother's book club as showcasing a certain kind of person: cruel, ill-informed, and lacking in artistic insight. There were, of course, notable exceptions. For one, my mother is herself quite adept when it comes to understanding complex literature, and though I feel like she could have spoken up and defended my work more rigorously, she did impress me with her insights and appreciations after the book club had dispersed. The other woman who surprised me with her sophisticated and discerning opinions was Molly, my ex-lover. In fact, Mother's book club's discussion of *The Emerald* is where Molly first showed up on my radar. I remember I was standing in the adjacent room, disheartened by the unexpected onslaught of cruel, baseless criticisms coming from my mother's senile friends, when a lone voice—softer and sweeter than the cackling of her colleagues—spoke up in dissent. "I'm surprised by your reactions," Molly said. "I enjoyed my time with the book. I found the writing to be just wonderful." I risked detection to poke my head around the corner and sneak a peek at my defender. That's when I laid eyes on Molly for the first time. I fell in love immediately.

25

Watch how Oscar Wilde reveals character in *The Picture of Dorian Gray*:

> Lord Henry elevated his eyebrows and looked at him in amazement through the thin blue wreaths of smoke that curled up in such fanciful whorls from his heavy, opium-tainted cigarette.

Now we know, through Wilde's clever and efficient use of detail, that the character has eyebrows. And notice how his cigarette is described as "heavy," which lets the reader know that Lord Henry is incredibly weak. We also learn, because of the blue smoke, that he's some kind of wizard character.

26

A character in your story can be a composite of different people you know. You might borrow certain characteristics from one person, and certain characteristics from another. For example, an important character in the novel I'm working on now was created using this technique. The character, Molly, borrows some elements from my ex-lover: her manner of speaking, her sense of humour, her looks. Her name, of course. She's from the same small town as Molly and had a similar family dynamic growing up. An ex-husband named Charles. Same interests and fears. But this character also wears a red beret, just like one of my neighbours. It's interesting to mash two different people together like this and see what happens.

27

Remember that your characters are human, and thus have human needs. You need to feed them regularly and keep them hydrated. Every few pages, have your character pull out a snack and sip from their water bottle. Accordingly, they require bathroom breaks. Has your character been running around for hours, talking to people and advancing the plot? They're likely pretty tired at this point—it's time for a nap. And if your protagonist hasn't been intimate with another character in a while, let the reader know how horny they've become. I don't know how many times I've been pulled out of a novel because the characters never seem to eat, sleep, or get really horny.

28

Names are important. When naming your character, one recommended approach is to look up the most popular baby names from the year and country they were born in, and pick at random from the list of results. There are a few caveats to keep in mind when employing this technique, however. First, if your character is a hippie, go ahead and give them a funny name like Potion or Saltine. Second, if your character is from Texas, it can be fun to call them Tex. Because of this, it's unwise to set your stories in the state of Texas; the great number of characters named Tex could get confusing for the reader. Third, if a character is a real historical figure—like Adolf Hitler or Babe Ruth—use their actual name. You don't need to make up a new name for a real person just because they're mentioned in a novel.

For stories set far in the future, you obviously can't consult a database of baby names from years that haven't happened yet, so use the hippie names. In the future we'll probably all have funny names like that. Those names will be considered normal then, though, so your characters shouldn't laugh at each other's names. Maybe you can have a character with a normal name like Steve, and everyone laughs at *him*. That could actually be pretty funny.

When choosing a surname, you want to clue the reader in to some significant trait or quality of the character. Think of Jack Reacher from Lee Child's novels: the name tells you how he's always "reaching" for things. It might seem silly and unnatural to have all of these characters running around with last names that literally say something about their personalities, however. To avoid this problem, you can disguise the names by making them Irish or Jewish. Here are some examples of meaningful, yet natural-sounding surnames:

Strongstein
O'Brave
Basketballberg

29

People like to read about characters they would want to have a beer with. They should be interesting, amiable, and basically the kind of individual you could imagine sitting down and having a beer with. Take, for example, the wide cast of characters who populate J. R. R. Tolkien's fantasy series *The Lord of the Rings*. I would sit down and have a beer with Frodo. Of course, I'd definitely want to have a beer with Gandalf. Samwise Gamgee—I'd have a beer. Merry and Pippin—beer. I'd sit down with Aragorn and have a beer, and I would also want to have a beer with Gimli. I would definitely want sit down and have a beer with Arwen. I'd have a beer with Elrond. I think we would all want to sit down and have a beer with the Ents. I'd also have a beer with Galadriel. Boromir, beer for sure. Legolas, beer. I'd even want to have a beer with Gollum. *That* would be interesting. And of course, you can't forget Bilbo Baggins. I'd want to sit down and have a beer with him too.

30

Learn to subvert the expectations readers will have for your characters. If every choice a character makes is the obvious, predictable choice, then the audience will become bored. If your protagonist is established as an experienced, well-respected surgeon, it could be interesting to show them saying things like: "I don't know how to perform surgery." If one of your characters is an environmentalist, let's see them gleefully burn down a forest. Have your decrepit old man character win the big foot race. Guess who's hosting a backyard tea party for all of the little dogs in the neighbourhood? A mean guy. Guess who assassinated the president? The president's friend. And, assuming you've been following this advice, guess who you now have in the palm of your hand?

The reader.

31

In a literary work, one or both of your protagonist's parents should be dead. Not only does this help make your character sympathetic and add emotional weight to their situation, it can actually help you work in exposition. Throughout a novel, a protagonist with a dead mother or father can visit their parent's grave and catch them up on the plot. And when your character talks to their dead parent's grave, they're not just talking to their dead parent. They're talking to the reader. You can take advantage of this and remind your audience of things that have happened in the book so far. "Well, Mother," your orphaned protagonist might say, "I managed to track Rusty's gang to their underground hideout and retrieve the prime minister's missing crown. Turns out the crown was actually a clever fake, but I received an anonymous tip on where to find the counterfeiter. Off to Bangkok!"

32

While first impressions are important, remember that a character doesn't need to fully reveal themselves to the reader during their first encounter. A character's background and quirks and various traits can be uncovered over time, throughout the course of your story. Think of how we learn about people in real life: we don't find out everything we need to know about a person the first time we meet them. This information is doled out over subsequent meetings. When I first saw Molly at my mother's book club, I only knew a few things: she had sophisticated artistic insights, she was beautiful, and I loved her. But I would learn so much more about her as time went on. I started attending Mom's book club regularly, listening from the other room, until I got up the courage to approach Molly on her way out of the building. I introduced myself, we spoke for a few minutes, and our little post–book club interactions became a regular occurrence. Eventually, I would ask Molly out on a date and I would learn even more about this fascinating woman. Her kindness, her gentle laugh. Her sweet tooth. That she could play any show tune on the piano. That she'd briefly lived in Hong Kong. That she was technically married, but she and Charles were basically living separate lives by the time we met. That she had a son who would've been older than me, but he had died in a traffic accident years earlier. That "old person smell" is really a myth. Molly had a wonderful scent. But I had to learn this over time.

33

The characters in your stories can actually be animals. One example of this is George Orwell's *Animal Farm*. I'm sure there are others. When experimenting with animal characters, however, it's important to remember that they see the world differently from humans. For instance, a lot of animals can see in the dark. Also, pets like cats and dogs are so much smaller than us, and so everything we think of as normal sized would actually be huge to them. Consider this short scene, written from the perspective of a cat:

> There's a mouse under that chair, the cat thought. If I sneak up behind the couch, climb the curtains, and quietly jump onto the table, maybe I can drop down and catch the mouse by surprise.

This is absurd. How are we supposed to believe that a cat is thinking these thoughts, when all of the details are described as if from a human's perspective? Now let's look at the scene again, revised to reflect the size of the cat narrator:

There's a huge mouse under that giant chair, the cat thought. If I sneak up behind the enormous couch, climb the huge curtains, and quietly jump onto the giant table, maybe I can drop down and catch the huge mouse by surprise.

34

Give your characters skills to help them deal with the various obstacles your plot will set in their path. Your protagonist should definitely have a driver's licence so they can get around, and it can open even more doors plot-wise if you give them a pilot's licence. A medical licence can be useful, too, in case they become injured. Establish that they're wealthy early on; while poor characters are often quite interesting to gawk at, the resources available to a rich character will simply give your story more narrative options. I suggest equipping your protagonist with a backpack full of basic supplies on page one, so that you have everything you need to get them out of trouble once it pops up. A good, story-minded backpack should contain a first aid kit, a flashlight, extra batteries, various maps, a compass, a passport, an electronic language translator, bug spray, bear spray, a knife, a handgun (with extra ammo), two bottles of water, two granola bars, condoms, a suicide pill, a can of Red Bull, night vision goggles, lip balm, a skeleton key that can open any door, and a blank cheque signed by Bill Gates.

35

When introducing your story's antagonist, you should never explicitly refer to them as "the antagonist." You need to use subtle hints and visual clues that will identify them as such. Tattoos and eye patches are commonly associated with villain types. A cigarette dangling from their lips will also work. Or a giant e-cigarette. Show your antagonist idly tossing a coin in the air. They should be staring into a cracked mirror, laughing. Give them sharpened teeth. A devilish grin—you need to actually write that it's a "devilish" grin, because a grin on its own is just a smile, which is something nice people do. What else? Their clothes can be those prison clothes with the stripes. And they should have bugs in their hair.

36

We get to know fictional characters in the same way we get to know the people in our lives. Every time you learn something about a stranger, however small, you start to build up a picture of them in your mind. That picture becomes more and more clear over time, as you gain further information. There comes a moment when this stranger is suddenly no longer a stranger—they are an acquaintance, or a friend, or a character in a novel that *feels like* an acquaintance or friend. For example, there's Abe, the esteemed editor of Ballast Books, who has taken an interest in my novel, *The Emerald*. I've never met Abe, and so I've constructed my impression of him based on a few email exchanges and whatever else I could glean from the internet. He won't friend me on Facebook, which is fine, but I can still see his profile picture. This depicts two people, a man and a woman, standing on a beach somewhere, holding hands. I assume that the man is Abe and that the woman is his partner. Now I can deduce he's in a long-term relationship. He enjoys visiting the beach. That's a start. And then, from the emails, I know he has great taste in books and can spot new literary talent. He's definitely going to take on *The Emerald*, and I think it's the perfect home for this important novel. Ballast Books is already held in high esteem, but I think *The Emerald* might further cement their reputation of publishing works of the finest quality. So you can see how I'm able to fill in the portrait of this man I haven't met yet, based on the small bit of information I have available at the moment. But I will meet Abe, probably soon. I could definitely see us becoming close friends. Talking shop over cold brewskis. Watching baseball games together, or whatever sport he prefers. Unless he's more of a film buff, in which case we could catch a movie. Maybe we could take a vacation together, like to that beautiful beach from his Facebook photo. I can't wait.

Details

37

Specificity is your best friend. The more your work is grounded in concrete detail, the more it will come alive for the reader. Your characters should never say "pass the ketchup." They should say "pass the Heinz." Specific, real-world details like this will electrify your stories and make them feel authentic. Consider this dull scene, which lacks specificity:

"I'm hungry, Ma," the boy said.

"We'll eat when we get to the mall," Susan said. "Put your coat on. We're late."

"Can I get pizza?"

"Hurry up. I'm going to start the car."

Now let's look at the scene again, this time revised to include specific details that breathe life into an otherwise unmemorable encounter:

"I'm hungry for McDonald's cheeseburgers, Susan Beeford," Max Beeford, Susan Beeford's eight-year-old son, said.

"We'll eat McDonald's cheeseburgers when we get to the

Westtown Shopping Plaza on Oxford Road," Susan Beeford (thirty-five years old) said. "Put your blue Eddie Bauer Men's CirrusLite Down Jacket on. We're late."

"Can I also get a medium three-topping pizza from Pizza Pizza?"

"Hurry up. I'm going to start the 2015 Infiniti QX80 LIMITED NAVIGATION/360 CAMERA/8 PASSENGER."

38

Small details and subtle hints can be used to build up a character in the reader's imagination. We see a man pushing a stroller down the street and assume that he is a new father. If that man's eyes are darting around in a suspicious way, we might now think that he has stolen a baby. But then, suddenly, the supposed kidnapper stops and presses a button on the stroller's handle. A full-grown man climbs out of the stroller and he looks exactly like the first man. Another doppelgänger climbs out, and another, and we see the original man pushing the button on the handle over and over again. Now we can infer that the stroller is actually a cloning machine, which creates a clone of the person who pushes the button on the stroller's handle as soon as they push it. With just a few understated details, we've already learned so much about this character.

39

Some people are naturally observant, whereas others tend to live a more internal life, ignoring the world going on around them to varying degrees. If you recognize yourself belonging to the latter category of person, the good news is that you can train yourself to pay more attention and, through this training, bring more sensory detail to your writing. Pick a spot, somewhere outside, where people tend to pass by—a park bench would be perfect. Sit down with your notebook for one hour and describe everything you notice. Don't neglect any of the five senses. What do you see happening around you? What sounds can you hear? What smells can you detect? If there's an unpleasant body odour in the air, and no one else is around, is it actually coming from you? Can you feel the wind blowing gently on your neck? Or is it a creep standing behind the bench? For taste, you'll need to bring something with you, like gum or a hot dog. But if you really take the time to log everything about your experience in the park, or whatever location you choose, someone reading your notes should have a pretty accurate idea of what that experience was like for you, and you can carry this skill over to your fiction.

When I first became interested in Molly, I would often sit on the bench in front of her building. I wanted an excuse to talk to her and luckily Molly's apartment building stood right next to my mother's. That meant I could bring Tupperware I'd borrowed from Mother or a book I'd meant to lend her with me, set up shop on the bench, and wait for Molly to come in or out of her building. When she did, I'd call out her name, feigning surprise, and explain that I was on my way to my mother's when I became overcome with fatigue, and saw her building's bench. Molly must have thought I had a vitamin deficiency, what with the number of times she found me "resting" there. But the point is that during these little stakeouts, waiting for Molly to emerge, I would sit and observe the physical space around me. Everything about that little parkette between Molly's building and the sidewalk is as clear to me as if I were sitting there now. The brown bush. The brown bench. One time I saw this yellow bird. It's all still there, burned into my brain in vivid detail.

40

Observe how Christopher Isherwood uses detail to create a sense of urgency in *A Berlin Diary*:

> In the corner, three sham mediaeval halberds (from a theatrical touring company?) are fastened together to form a hatstand. Frl. Schroeder unscrews the heads of the halberds and polishes them from time to time. They are heavy and sharp enough to kill.

Isherwood knows he's presenting a rather dull scene, where we're kind of poking around this old apartment and there's no real action, so to keep things interesting for the reader he introduces home décor fashioned from weaponry. Even if a weapon isn't being used, it still draws our attention and makes us nervous that it *could* be used. And if it seems out of place to have weapons lying around everywhere in your story, you can go the Isherwood route and have weapons that are actually furniture. Spice up your character's homes with a gun chandelier, a painting that's really just a framed knife, or a toilet filled with poison.

41

I've mentioned that I share an apartment with my uncle Herman, and that he is mentally ill. Knowing that he's crazy, what do you picture his bedroom looking like? Perhaps you imagine that his floor is covered with trash and that he has strange notes posted all over the walls. That there are piss jars, dead bugs, and burn marks on the carpet. Maybe you would expect to find tinfoil over the window or some kind of unsettling shrine dedicated to a famous actress. In fact, the image you're conjuring is probably closer to what my room looks like, and I'm perfectly sane. My uncle's room is actually neat and tidy. All he has in there is a dresser for his clothes and a giant roll of brown packing paper. Every night he tears off a section of packing paper to sleep on, and another section to use as a blanket. One of my daily chores is to throw the previous night's paper down the trash chute, so it doesn't all pile up. The lesson here is that people don't always conform to your idea of how they must live, according to prevailing stereotypes. Insane people can have clean, uncluttered bedrooms.

42

Let's say you're writing a scene that takes place in a cemetery. The protagonist is attending a funeral and everyone is gathered at the gravesite, listening to the eulogy. Your natural impulse might be to say that it's also raining. Rainy weather could further evoke the sombre mood you're going for with this funeral scene. But what if it's actually nice and sunny in the graveyard? *Now* we have something interesting.

43

When you look back on important, pivotal moments in your life, the scenes playing out in your memory are likely filled to the brim with sensory detail. Remembering your first day of high school, perhaps you recall the smell of French fries in the cafeteria or the sound of the crackling PA system during morning announcements. The emotions we felt so strongly at the time are tied to these sensory details, so that when you encounter a similar smell to your high school cafeteria later in life, you might recall the feeling of nervous anticipation you felt on your first day of high school. In fiction, your characters are hopefully navigating emotionally heightened situations, and the rendering of these situations should be littered with the kind of sensory detail that binds itself to our emotional experiences. When I look back on the moment that I first asked Molly out on a date, I don't remember the exact words I said. Something about how it was pleasant running into her outside her building every now and then, but it would be nice to sit down over a meal and have a real conversation. I don't remember what Molly said in response, either. Obviously, she said yes, but I can't recall her phrasing.

What I do remember is looking at her hands and noticing for the first time how wrinkled and old looking they were. Because of Molly's wonderful fashion sense and her talent for applying makeup, she never really looked her age, but her hands told the truth. I became fixated on them. They looked like two grey balloons that had been deflated. Just kind of hanging from her sleeves, wobbling in the breeze. I remember this feeling in the pit of my stomach, like I had made a mistake. The generational gap between us was too pronounced. Now I had to go out for dinner with this woman and her ancient, ghoulish hands. What had I gotten myself into? Luckily, I didn't cancel our date and we ended up having a wonderful time. But when I bring up the memory of asking Molly to dinner—a textbook emotionally heightened situation—the sensory details are what stand out for me. I don't remember the exact content of our conversation, which launched what would eventually become a powerful, meaningful relationship. What comes into sharp focus are those sickly, withered hands.

44

When it comes to setting, sometimes less is more. Spending paragraph after paragraph describing every little detail of the character's surroundings at the beginning of each scene is rather old-fashioned, and a great way to bore your reader. An easy method to avoid this is to simply set your scenes in a Starbucks coffee shop. Every Starbucks is basically the same, and so you don't need to spend any time describing the environment. Just write "Starbucks" and the reader will know exactly what it looks like in there. For the same reason, you can also use famous landmarks and monuments as settings. If your protagonist travels from a Starbucks to the Eiffel Tower, back to Starbucks, then to the Grand Canyon, then Starbucks, and so on, you won't have to waste any precious space describing everything like some idiot from the Victorian era.

45

A story's setting can reveal interesting things about your characters. Individuals from a diverse range of backgrounds will all interact with and experience the very same environment differently. If a story is set in a garbage dump, a snooty, rich character will walk around in disgust. They will hate it there and might actually throw up. A poor character, however, won't mind it at all and think it's just a normal place.

46

Use your environment. The setting shouldn't simply be a backdrop that could be swapped out for any other backdrop without affecting the story in any meaningful way. The setting ought to be an active participant in the narrative. If your characters are on a baseball field, they should be playing baseball. If a scene takes place on a golf course, same thing: have your characters pick up clubs and make use of the setting. If your characters are simply standing in the middle of a race track having a conversation, why set your story there at all? Put them inside the cars and have them race around.

47

Let's say you're writing a scene set in a restaurant. Think of all
the different details that could potentially be included in your
scene: the size of the restaurant, how crowded or empty it is, the
music, the smells coming from the kitchen, the server's outfit,
the server's manner of speaking, the décor, the style and quality
of the cuisine, the font used on the menu, how far the bathroom
stall doors are from the ground, etc. You could go on for pages
and pages, describing every little thing about the restaurant, but
of course you need to be selective. What details make it into your
story, and what gets ignored? One striking detail can sometimes
tell the reader everything they need to know about a setting.
For example, an efficient writer might describe their restaurant
as having candles on the tables. Immediately, you can picture this
restaurant and understand that it's a "fancy" place. Or perhaps
the writer has their protagonist walk up to a counter and order
a Clown Burger with Silly Fries—a clear vision of this restaurant
instantly springs forth.

   With the novel I'm currently working on, the novel about my
relationship with Molly, I'm writing a scene inspired by our first

date, which took place at a restaurant. I had been ruminating over what details to include to accurately convey the setting, and I ended up focusing in on one evocative detail: when the server seated us at our table, I noticed that the tablecloth was actually a big sheet of paper and there were crayons set out for us to use. Can't you picture this restaurant perfectly? I remember feeling embarrassed at first: the place was called Albert's Steakhouse & Pizza, which I thought would be fancier and more romantic, because they used the name Albert instead of Al. But the crayons ended up being useful throughout the date, as I used them to draw notes and diagrams on the paper tablecloth that helped illustrate my points concerning the composition of *The Emerald*, which ended up being the main focus of our dinner conversation. I wish I could have taken the tablecloth home afterwards as a memento, but I ended up spilling my entire Sprite on it. In my novel, however, there will be no such spill. The protagonist will successfully (and covertly) take the tablecloth home and gift it to the Molly character years later, on their first wedding anniversary, at the end of the book. Boy, I wish I had that tablecloth to surprise Molly with once we get back together. But you see how with one small detail, I've not only conveyed the atmosphere and ambiance of an entire restaurant, but also sowed the seeds of a powerful, romantic conclusion to my novel. In the hands of a writer who knows what they're doing, something as seemingly insignificant as a tablecloth can end up becoming the spiritual heart of a novel. In fact, I may even title this book *The Tablecloth*. That's actually pretty good.

48

Let's look at Alice Munro's masterful use of detail in her story *Royal Beatings*:

> Flo had saved up, and had a bathroom put in, but there was no place to put it except in a corner of the kitchen. The door did not fit, the walls were only beaverboard. The result was that even the tearing of a piece of toilet paper, the shifting of a haunch, was audible to those working or talking or eating in the kitchen.

There's a lot going on here, but let's focus on perhaps the most interesting detail: the beaverboard. What the hell is beaverboard? you might ask. I'm not sure, and I don't think we're supposed to really know. Most likely, Munro invented something called "beaverboard" to jazz up her sentence. This is an important lesson: you can come up with new words in order to titillate and amuse your reader. Imagine you're describing the objects in a room: there's a flute, a knife, and a telephone. The knife is somewhat interesting, but otherwise this is pretty dull. Now imagine that the room contains a horseflute, a catknife, and a birdphone—suddenly, I'm paying attention. Let me into that room!

49

An oft-repeated piece of writing advice is "show, don't tell," and it's repeated for good reason. We should be able to intuit how a character is feeling from their actions—not because the narrator explicitly tells us. Instead of writing "he was angry," have the character stomp around the room, smashing everything and screaming. Instead of writing "she was confused," show us that she's scratching the top of her head with her index finger, her eyes crossed, drool pouring out of her open mouth. If a male character finds another character attractive, don't tell us. *Show us* his boner.

50

Consider the use of detail in Isaac Bashevis Singer's *Gimpel the Fool*:

> I entered the house. Lines were strung from wall to wall and
> clothes were drying. Barefoot she stood by the tub, doing the
> wash. She was dressed in a worn hand-me-down gown of plush.
> She had her hair put up in braids and pinned across her head.
> It took my breath away, almost, the reek of it all.

Notice how all of these specific, concrete details converge
to show the reader that this character is quite poor. Instead of
saying "she's poor," Singer is instead able to accomplish this
simple sentiment with several lines of description. This can be
a clever way to drive up the word count if you're having a hard
time coming up with stuff for your characters to do.

51

One small detail can change everything. The thrift department store where I work, for example, has terrible lighting. It makes pretty much everyone look hideous. A supermodel could walk into the store, and I'd barely get aroused. One time, Molly came to visit me at work and I almost broke up with her on the spot. Jesus, I thought, *this* is who I'm dating? This weathered crone? Thankfully, I bit my tongue and instead asked her to never come by my work again, because the manager had a weird rule about romantic partners not being allowed in the store. Soon the grotesque image of Molly standing under the harsh lights of Value Village faded, and I learned a valuable lesson: always scout out a potential date location's lighting situation before taking Molly there. And that one small detail can really change everything.

52

When conducting research for your stories, consider the reliability of the sources you are using. Mainstream media outlets are often compromised by their ties to corporate interests and so shouldn't be trusted. I prefer to seek out journalism that isn't swayed by big business, like the Reality Check Justice Network channel on YouTube. Trent Bachman, the host of the Reality Check Justice Network's flagship daily news roundup tells it like it is, refusing to accept the truth-skewing corporate payouts regularly received by media conglomerates. No other news source was brave enough to take on the truth behind big kale. Trent showed how pharmaceutical companies, in league with the Farmers of America, regularly conspire to test new drugs on an unwitting public by dosing certain crops and then pushing this food on the population with an intense grassroots campaign of public persuasion. When American kale was fortified with a new sleeping aid called Prenium-X, hundreds of people all over the world became victim to one of the experimental drug's most dangerous side effects: spontaneous combustion. There's an incredible spike in reports of people "randomly" exploding, starting exactly around the time kale's popularity jumped. You can look this up on Reality Check Justice Network's channel—it's all there. So you want to consider your sources carefully before incorporating research into your work.

53

Here's what an afternoon of research might look like: you head
to the public library and start moving from shelf to shelf. Let's
say you're writing about the American Civil War. You scour the
history section, pluck out several volumes. There are books pro-
viding a general overview of the conflict, detailed biographies of
important figures, oral histories and letters from the era, critical
essays, etc. You then find an empty table and set the books down
in front of you, along with a notebook and pen. Now forget about
the Civil War. Look around you: there's a man using one of
the library's computers, boldly browsing pornography. There's
a woman sleeping in her chair. And there's another man on a
computer, also browsing pornography. *This* is what you should
really be writing about—these perverts.

54

One of the wonderful things about being a writer in the modern age is having the ability to conduct research from home, using the internet. As long as you are able to discern reliable sources, you could conceivably learn everything there is to know about most subjects with a few mouse clicks. I've mentioned Abe, the esteemed editor of Ballast Books who is interested in possibly acquiring *The Emerald*. Recently, I happened upon his eleven-year-old son Patrick's Instagram account. I browsed through his photos, looking to see if the family was possibly on a long trip, which would account for Abe not responding to my emails, but all I found were pictures of Patrick's extensive Pokémon card collection. How disappointing, I thought. Later that evening, however, I realized that I could use Patrick's Pokémon obsession to my advantage. If I were to establish an online friendship with Patrick, I'd have a direct line into Abe's household. Perhaps Patrick could help me convince his father to publish my novel. I just needed Patrick to think I knew a lot about Pokémon stuff. I dove into research mode immediately: I scoured the internet and learned everything I could about Pokémon and Pokémon cards. I learned which characters were popular and what rare cards collectors fought over. It only took me a few hours, and then I created my own Instagram account devoted to Pokémon cards. I sent Patrick a follow request and, the next day, he accepted. I sent him a direct message immediately: "Hi, Patrick! I've been admiring your collection. Would love to trade with you!" Later that day, my research paid off. Patrick wrote back "cool." Soon enough, I'll have Abe's son working for me and a publishing contract with Ballast Books will be within reach. Writing a great book is only half the battle—you also need to work the business side of things if you want to find literary success.

Plot

55

A story without conflict is no story at all. Conflict is the fuel that drives everything. Tattoo the word "conflict" onto your forearm, if that's what it takes for you to remember the importance of conflict in fiction. To create conflict, think of what your character is afraid of most and place that fear directly in front of them. If a character is afraid of snakes, they should stumble upon a snake den. If a character is afraid of heights, stick them on top of a skyscraper and watch what happens. If you're having trouble bringing enough conflict into your work, remember that everyone is afraid of murderers. If you include a murderer in your story, all of your characters will definitely be afraid and you will have more than enough conflict.

56

While we all face adversity in our lives to varying degrees, characters in novels tend to find themselves mired in constant conflict, almost to the point of absurdity. This is because, without conflict, there would be no story to tell. One of the reasons I've decided to write a novel based on my relationship with Molly is that conflict followed us around at every step. When we first started seeing each other, we had to keep our courtship a secret. Though she had moved into her own apartment by this point, Molly was still technically married and didn't want people to gossip. And then there was the whole May-December thing we had going on. While neither of us actually cared about our age difference, we didn't want the prying eyes and judgements of others to spoil the carefree fun that comes with a new relationship. That Molly lived in the building next to my mother's meant I had to be extra cautious when visiting my new girlfriend. We both knew that Mother would disapprove of us dating. I purchased a fake beard to facilitate visiting Molly undetected, which gave me an unsightly rash. My apartment was even trickier, since Uncle Herman was almost always home and spoke on the phone regularly to my mother. He would surely spill the beans. Because of all this, most of our meet-ups occurred at Albert's Steakhouse & Pizza. Not only was the restaurant conveniently located in between our two neighbourhoods, but I found that the paper tablecloth and free crayons facilitated our literary discussions, since I could jot down important points and draw diagrams to help illustrate my ideas. Much of the material for this writing guide was conceived in rough form on those tablecloths. The food was decent, too. Free Sprite refills. Albert's became *our place*. I miss going there. God, if I could only meet Molly in our special booth tonight and we could pick up where we left off. I guess I'll have to be patient. But you can see how our situation, having to sneak around and avoid detection, would make for an exciting narrative. Fill your story with obstacles and your plot will have enough fuel to carry your characters to the end. Maybe I'll go to Albert's tonight, by myself. It will be hard, but could help me process things. Sometimes I miss being with Molly so much that my entire body hurts. This has been a painful year for me.

57

How should your story begin? It can help to look at classic works to see how accomplished writers kick off their narratives. Here's Henry James with the first sentence of *Washington Square*:

> During a portion of the first half of the present century, and more particularly during the latter part of it, there flourished and practised in the city of New York, a physician who enjoyed perhaps an exceptional share of the consideration which, in the United States, has always been bestowed upon distinguished members of the medical profession.

At first, this may seem like a bit of a snooze. The narrator sounds like a snivelling dweeb reciting their book report. When I read "perhaps an exceptional share of the consideration," I immediately want to stick my head in the toilet and drown myself. But why, then, do I keep reading? I keep reading because James, the scoundrel, has snuck something in there, amidst all of the pretentious rambling: New York. What I thought was going to be a novel about this insufferable twat yammering on and on, is actually about the greatest city in the world. New York City, baby! Now we're talking Times Square, *Saturday Night Live*, and "I'm walkin' here."

58

Many writers utilize something called a "story circle" during the planning stages of their novels, to help figure out the plot. A story circle is when you draw a big circle and then write everything that happens to your characters inside the circle. I haven't found this to be all that helpful myself, but it may work for you.

59

Joseph Campbell described a popular narrative pattern called the Hero's Journey, which many writers use as a template for plot structure. Essentially, the "hero" is called to adventure, they journey into a supernatural realm, and eventually return home bearing gifts. The hero in the story needn't be Superman, however. They don't even have to be a firefighter or emergency room doctor. They can be a novelist who dates an older woman. And the journey doesn't have to be one where the hero travels to outer space or the lost city of Atlantis. They don't have to go anywhere. The journey can simply be that something changes about the hero. The writer and the old woman go through a break-up—that's the journey. And if the novelist and the old woman end up getting back together, that's *two* Hero's Journeys. This Molly novel is really shaping up to be something special. It would actually be insane if I couldn't find a publisher for it.

60

If you find yourself stuck and can't figure out how to make your plot move forward, try placing your protagonist in the exact situation they've been trying to avoid throughout your novel thus far. One afternoon, in the early days of my relationship with Molly, while we were still trying to keep everything a secret, we were almost caught by my uncle Herman. He had a doctor's appointment and was supposed to be out of the apartment for a few hours, so I invited Molly over. Minutes after Molly arrived, however, Herman came back in a huff—he'd decided that his doctor was planning to insert a mind-control chip into his thyroid gland and so he cancelled the appointment. He looked over at Molly, who was sitting on the couch, and I knew I couldn't tell him the truth. He would tell my mother, and she'd start asking questions. Poking her nose into my business. I had to improvise. "Darn it all," I said. "You spoiled the surprise! I hired a cleaning woman to make the place nice for you." I then took my uncle out for lunch while poor Molly had to spend two hours dusting, vacuuming, and scrubbing our apartment. I felt bad for her, but I was proud of the way I was able to think on my feet. Molly actually did a wonderful job with the cleaning. Our place never looked so nice, and now the "plot" that Molly and I found ourselves caught up in was able to move forward.

61

A successful story will always have rising action. This is where the conflict steadily increases as the narrative progresses. Let's say your protagonist encounters a poison balloon–wielding assassin in the first few chapters. The next time these two characters meet, the assassin should hand your protagonist two poison balloons. Eventually, you can build up to the assassin filling your protagonist's home with a whole truckload of poison balloons. Then perhaps the assassin comes flying toward your protagonist in a hot air balloon that's actually filled with poisonous gas. And finally, in the climax, the assassin replaces the Earth's atmosphere with poisonous gas and the protagonist has to stick his head inside a normal, oxygen-filled balloon in order to survive. Aim for a natural escalation of conflict like this in your work, and your readers will stick around until the end of the story.

62

In terms of plot, you need to hold off playing your biggest hand until the final act. You want to lead the reader to this climax slowly, building tension with each scene until you can eventually deliver your final blow: the story's most exciting, dramatic sequence. I previously related the story of how I'd befriended Ballast Books editor Abe's son Patrick over Instagram, and how I was pretending to be a Pokémon card collector in order to hopefully use him to persuade his father to publish my novel. So far, I've been proposing low-level trades with Patrick, offering him decent, but not especially rare cards in exchange for whatever cards I know he has multiple copies of. I lied and said I live in San Francisco, which is where he lives, and can meet him at his school during recess to conduct the big trade once we work out the particulars. He said "ok." Gradually, however, I plan on sweetening the deal: offering better, rarer cards that I know he doesn't have in his collection. Really get him on the hook. And then, a few days before the trade is supposed to take place, I'll drop a bombshell on him: I'll offer up a 1999 First Edition Shadowless Holographic Charizard #4. An extremely rare and expensive Pokémon card, and he doesn't even have to give up any of his own cards. All he has to do is walk into his daddy's office, locate a manuscript titled *The Emerald*, and put it in his own bedroom. When his father discovers it, Patrick will recite a script I've written for him about how he happened upon the novel and was instantly captivated by my prose. He'll go on and on about how much he adored the book and how all his friends would love it too. That it has universal appeal and could work in several different markets. Obviously, I don't have a 1999 First Edition Shadowless Holographic Charizard #4, but that doesn't matter. Once Patrick talks his father into publishing my book, I'll delete the Instagram account and all of our interactions will disappear without a trace. It's a devilishly clever plan, and the whole thing works exactly like the plot of a successful story. Instead of coming on too strong and offering my best Pokémon card right away, which could arouse suspicion, I'm building up to it and gaining Patrick's trust, just like how a novelist needs to slowly gain the trust of their readers to build toward that final, climactic scene.

63

Another important aspect of plotting is the denouement. Ah, the denouement! When everything comes together in this certain way and it's all just so *denouement*. It's hard to describe exactly, but you know denouement when you see it. It's kind of later in the story and everything just has this sort of quality, and it's all put together in a way that has this *je ne sais quoi*.

64

An exciting way to begin your story is *in media res*. Latin for "in the middle of things," *in media res* beginnings begin in the middle of things. Instead of setting up exposition to explain where we are and what's happening, you can drop the reader right into the centre of the action. This technique will grab the reader's attention. To do this, write your story normally, with a tepid, exposition-heavy beginning. Later, go back and find the first exciting action scene in the story. Cut everything that comes before this scene. Now the story starts with a compelling event, instead of whatever dull sequence you originally wanted to kick things off with. So that you don't waste all of that introductory prose you spent so much time working on, you can paste in the excised writing later in the story. Simply preface this cut material with something like: "Paul was bored, so he decided to close his eyes and enjoy some of his memories." Now you can put back in all of the stuff you cut, because the protagonist is having a flashback. Don't forget to signal to the reader when this sequence is finished: "Paul opened his eyes and returned to the present; his big flashback was over."

65

Is the greatest story of all time found in one of the holy books, like Moses parting the Red Sea? No, it is not. What about one of the classic folktales that have endured through the ages? Guess again. What about Homer's *The Odyssey*? Or something by Shakespeare? Sorry, but no. The greatest story of all time is the one where the guy sells his dead kid's shoes.

66

Think of your novel's plot in terms of cause and effect. Events shouldn't just happen—they should be the result of your character's decisions. An effective way to ensure this is to replace all of the "and thens" in your story outline with "therefores." Let's say, in your outline, you write "Paul eats an ice cream cone and then he robs a bank." Now change this to "Paul eats an ice cream cone and *therefore* he robs a bank." The revised version is an example of successful cause-and-effect plotting, since now we know Paul robs the bank *because* he ate the ice cream cone. It's not some random event that Paul robs the bank: his decision to rob the bank is a direct result of him eating an ice cream cone, and the scene where Paul robs the bank will now feel earned.

67

A story's plot is the vessel that will carry your characters to a place where they are able to change. At the beginning of a novel, the protagonist should find themselves in some kind of rut. The only way out of this rut is for the protagonist to make it through the series of hazardous events laid out for them in the book. If they are able to do this, they will transform.

At the time of writing this, I myself am stuck in a bit of a rut: Molly has left me, Abe from Ballast Books won't respond to my emails, and it's getting harder and harder to get out of bed in the morning. Looking at my situation through the lens of a fiction writer, however, I can see a clear path forward. To escape my rut and truly change, I need to overcome obstacles. I need to deal with the conflict in my path, just like the characters in my stories would. I can't sit around, waiting for change to come to me; that's the passive route, which guarantees narrative death. I must take up an active role and confront my obstacles. I will continue to email Abe, work on his young son over Instagram, and maybe I can even track down a phone number. I will frequent the bench in front of Molly's building, just as I did when

I first became infatuated with her, and wait for her to pass by. I will drop to my knees, beg for her forgiveness, and convince her to take me back. I'll write her poetry—love poetry—and slip it under her door. I've never written poetry before, but poetry is kid's stuff to a novelist, and I will certainly excel at the form.

Sitting around feeling sorry for myself won't accomplish anything. I need to earn the change I desire. I need to be more like the protagonists in the stories I write. Which is kind of funny because the protagonist of the story I'm writing now, the Molly novel, is *me*. So I'm aspiring to be more like a character who is already based on me. That's some trippy, postmodern, metafiction stuff, and I now see that this is the route the Molly novel must take. The Molly novel can be about me trying to write about my relationship with Molly, but also how I'm envious of the main character of the novel, who is actually me, and how these different mirrored selves all sort of collapse into each other. And the narrative can be told backwards. Or the timeline can kind of loop around and feed back into itself, like a Möbius strip. Maybe the reader can somehow be an active character in the novel? Wait until you see *this* one, Abe.

68

The climax is the point in a story where the conflict and tension reach their highest level. Here, the protagonist finally faces the story's main antagonist, or solves the novel's central problem. In a murder mystery, the climax comes when the detective finally uncovers and confronts the killer. In a story about an assassin who uses poison balloons to dispatch his victims, the climax occurs when the assassin accidentally poisons himself with his own poison balloon. A Batman story reaches its climax, say, when Batman finally solves the Riddler's big riddle and then kills the Riddler. Without a climax, the story won't reach a dramatic conclusion and things will just sort of peter out. "Peter out" is a funny expression: *I hope I don't peter out. I'm petering out right now. I can't stop petering out over here.*

69

A note about endings: you don't have to actually write "THE END" at the end of a literary work. The reader should turn to the next page, expecting more story, and instead find the author's acknowledgements, which is like a pre-emptive award acceptance speech that writers toss in to lend their books an air of prize-winnery.

Style

70

There are essentially two factors that will determine a writer's prose style. The first is sentence length. Will the writer express themselves in short, terse sentences, or long and winding ones? The second factor relates to vocabulary. Some authors like to include highfalutin words like "tumultuous," while others use cuss words like "shitbag" and "piss." If you lean toward short sentences and cuss words, you have a Tough Guy style. Like Hemingway. Using longer sentences and fancy words indicates an Egghead style—think Henry James. Writers either have a Tough Guy style, an Egghead style, or a rare Tough Egg style, which is a hybrid of the two. The Tough Egg style might look something like this:

"Come back here at once, you tumultuous shitbag!"

I can't think of any famous writers who fall neatly into this category, off the top of my head. It's not easy to pull off. I actually write with this Tough Egg style and some might argue that I'm a pioneering figure of the Tough Egg school of writing. But it's quite difficult to execute Tough Egg successfully, and so I recommend sticking with one of the other two, less demanding styles.

71

Every writer should work on building up their vocabulary. The more tools you have at your disposal, the more creative options you will have. Even if you tend to write in a simple style, having access to a greater range of words will give your writing more precision. I recommend purchasing several word-a-day calendars to help grow your vocabulary. You can find a wide variety of word-a-day calendars on the internet for pretty cheap, and you don't have to buy them from the current year. You don't have to wait for the next day to learn a new word, either: you can just read through the calendars like a normal book. There are several word-a-day calendars piled up on my nightstand right now. When I go to the beach, I often bring a small stack of calendars and enjoy them the way others enjoy paperback thrillers. Some of my most cherished books are calendars. That's why my vocabulary is now so *effervescent* and *palatial*.

72

There are several distinct methods of storytelling available to writers, which are called modes. These different modes can be switched between throughout a work of fiction, adding variety to the proceedings and causing many interesting narrative effects. Let's now look at some of the individual modes, supplemented by excerpts from my Molly novel-in-progress, which I've included in order to illustrate what each mode looks like in the hands of a seasoned pro.

EXPOSITION: This mode is used to insert background information necessary within the story. Writing instructors often warn their students to "show, don't tell" when it comes to narration, but exposition is all about the "telling," which is sometimes necessary to set up plot or clarify different story elements.

The nature of Molly's fractured relationship with her husband was unclear to me at first, but over the course of several dates and conversations, the fog slowly lifted and I learned how their marriage fell apart. They'd been together for forty-four years and were married for forty-two of those, by the time I came into the picture. Molly met Charles at her cousin Bernice's wedding. Charles was friends with the groom. They were seated at the same table and ended up hitting it off. Charles made a good first impression on Molly—he usually does, with naive types. He often comes across as nice, genial, and polite, if a little dull. But sometimes "being nice" is just a cover. What, then, was Charles hiding behind his polite facade? Even more dullness, it turned out. Charles was so boring that spending time with the man could almost be considered assault. And it was this violent capacity for dullness which, over the years, pounded Molly into the ground and nearly sapped the life from her.

DESCRIPTION: This is where vivid imagery and sensory details are used to illustrate the physical world of the story. You don't want to get bogged down with too much description, as this can bore the reader, but sometimes it's important to enter this narrative mode in order to bring a fictional world to life.

The first time I saw a photograph of Molly's husband, I almost threw up. Unlike Molly, Charles did *not* age gracefully. An absolute ghoul. A tinge of grey to his skin, and folds under his eyes like a pile of T-shirts at the Gap. One of his ears looked messed up. Weak jaw. Something was just generally off about him. You know how you can almost tell that someone has offensive breath from the way they look? I try not to judge people based on their appearance, but as soon as I saw Charles's face, I knew that he was a bad person.

ACTION: In this mode, the narration focuses in on physical movement. The characters navigate through their surroundings and interact with the environment. Action scenes generally have a faster pace than the other modes, and can be rather exciting for the reader.

I waited outside Charles's house for hours. The ghillie suit was punishingly hot, but nobody would be able to see me in the bushes. I wondered what Charles would do if he discovered me there. "I'm looking out for Molly," I'd say. "I need to know if you're going to be a threat. See what I'm dealing with here." If he tried to attack me, I'd jump to the side. Then, utilizing the momentum from Charles's own attack against him, I'd push him into the grass with a palm strike to the spine. Then I'd step on one of his wrists and grab the other arm, twisting it. He'd be completely incapacitated at that point. But if he had a weapon in his hand, I'd focus on disarming him first. Kick the knife from his hand with a roundhouse. Then put him in a half nelson. He wouldn't stand a chance. Even if he had a gun, I could drop to the ground, out of firing range, and sweep his legs. Grab the gun. Half nelson. Game over, Charles.

INTROSPECTION: This mode is for when your protagonist needs to stop and reflect on things that have happened thus far, or ruminate on future plans. Sometimes it can be useful to allow your characters a chance to take stock of a situation and analyze their own motivations.

I stood in Charles's driveway, peering through his living room window at a heartbreaking scene. Charles sat there, alone, watching what appeared to be an old home movie of him and Molly camping. It was hard to see clearly from that distance, but I could tell that they were pretty young in the video—it could've been their honeymoon. I knew from Molly that Charles was still hung up on her. Now I was witnessing the proof. Am I doing the right thing, I wondered, pursuing a relationship with Molly? What if I was out of the picture and they were able to patch things up and get back together? Am I the reason that this poor, pathetic man is probably wracked with pain and longing right now? Am I actively ruining his life? And, perhaps, Molly's life too?

No, I realized. Everything I'm doing is fine.

DIALOGUE: This is pretty self-explanatory. I'll be covering dialogue more extensively in a later chapter, but here's an example from the Molly novel for consistency's sake:

"I miss him so much," Molly said.

"I know," Molly's sister, Carole, said. "He's the love of your life."

"He really is. I can't believe I was married to that moron Charles for so long. And now that I've actually found my dream guy, I've thrown it all away. Do you think Sam will take me back?"

"Of course he will."

"At least I have his brilliant writing to keep me company. I've been reading *The Emerald* over and over again. It's just so tremendous. Did you get a chance to read it yet?"

"Yes, I did. And I was floored. There's no question that he's a genius."

"Absolutely, no question."

73

Writers are often told to avoid using the passive voice. This can be tricky, however. To illustrate, here is the Wikipedia definition of passive voice:

> In a clause with passive voice, the grammatical subject express-es the theme or patient of the main verb—that is, the person or thing that undergoes the action or has its state changed. This contrasts with active voice, in which the subject has the agent role.

The problem, obviously, is that this is incredibly confusing. What does "patient of the main verb" even mean? Luckily, there's a solution: The Professor.

The Professor is a smart character you can bring in to dismiss or counteract specific criticisms someone might direct toward your work. If you're not sure what passive voice means, and therefore cannot be sure you are not using it in your story, have The Professor step in and declare with authority that the use of passive voice in literature is perfectly fine. It might look some-thing like this:

"Boy, I sure was enjoying this novel," Paul said, "but the author keeps using the passive voice. That's bad."

"Actually," The Professor said, "there's nothing wrong with using the passive voice. Me and my colleagues at Ivy League University use it frequently. Anyway, gotta go."

74

Diction is important for establishing a story's overall tone. There are several different language styles a writer can choose from when composing a work of fiction:

EDITED: Not too loose, not too formal. This is the industry standard. Because this style is so overused, I would avoid it.

FORMAL: Stuffy and pretentious. Avoid.

COLLOQUIAL: Avoid this as well—much too casual and loose.

REGIONAL: Taking on regional expressions and speaking patterns can be distracting, and sometimes insulting, so I would avoid.

NON-STANDARD: Makes use of dialects and slang. Too informal, can also be insulting. Avoid.

CAVEMAN: Simulating Neanderthal speech could be pretty interesting, and you don't see it a lot. Probably your most viable option.

75

A good sense of rhythm is crucial in fiction. The words that come together to make up your story should flow together and feel effortlessly musical and pleasing to the reader. The most effective way to make sure your work flows well is to read it aloud. Again, and again. As you work through a new paragraph, and after the tenth or twentieth edit, read it out. Just looking at your sentences on a page or computer screen won't give you a good sense of the story's rhythm. I often record myself reading my work aloud and then play the recordings on a loop while I'm sleeping. This technique allows my subconscious mind to absorb the rhythmic patterns of my stories and establish what needs to be tweaked. If nothing else, listening to these recordings can lead to interesting story ideas: one night, I awoke to a recording of myself reading through the previous day's work and I thought that an intruder was in my room, speaking to me. And for a brief moment, in my hazy state of half-sleep, I thought that the intruder was *me*. That I had somehow split into two identical beings and that my corporeal copy was now confronting me in my bed. This strange experience inspired my short story "The Doppelgänger," which I actually sent to *The New Yorker*. They recently wrote back with a rejection, but I was elated to see that it was the "good" rejection form letter. They send this good rejection letter when they admire a story and the editor fought to place it in the magazine, but there simply wasn't room. You can tell when you've received the good letter because the tone is a little softer and more encouraging. The thing with *The New Yorker* is that they have so many editors and receive so many submissions that you can send the same story to them over and over again and nobody will notice. So a story is never truly rejected by them, because you can keep submitting it until one of the editors gives it the green light. And now that "The Doppelgänger" has elicited the much sought-after good rejection form letter, it's only a matter of time before I get that green light.

76

The pace of a story can determine whether or not readers will stick with a narrative until the very end. If a story's pace is too slow, the reader will become bored. If it's too fast, the reader will become exhausted. The trick is to move back and forth between fast- and slow-paced scenes, which will help manage the reader's levels of boredom and exhaustion. After an exciting, fast-paced scene full of action and exciting developments, transition into a slow, dull scene so that the reader can trance out for a bit. Television shows are regularly interrupted by commercial breaks, which give the viewers a chance to use the washroom or just sit there and not have to think about what's happening on screen for a few minutes. Literature doesn't have that built-in safeguard against audience fatigue, so it's important to plug in these tedious moments every few pages. Think of *Moby Dick*, an American literary classic: Melville knew that his seafaring adventure story would overstimulate his readers if he didn't include monotonous and uninteresting asides throughout the novel. That's why we get these long digressions about whaling equipment and zoological classifications in between all the fun harpoon fights.

77

Avoid using clichés in your work. Every cliché started out as an expression meant to convey an idea in a clear, interesting, and original manner, which is actually your job as a writer. You should be coming up with new clichés, not keeping the old ones alive. One effective way to create an original cliché is to modify a classic. Here are some examples of well-established clichés that I have edited into bold new expressions:

OLD	NEW
Happy as a clam.	Happy as a clown.
Kill two birds with one stone.	Kill two birds with one big knife.
Look what the cat dragged in!	Look what the clown dragged in!

78

Here's another cliché: "my heart is broken." This one is so ubiquitous that most people don't even realize what they're saying. You can't break your heart. You break your bones. And as someone whose heart is actually (figuratively) broken right now, I can tell you that the expression isn't accurate. It's more like both my arms are broken, because breaking both my arms would be so painful and inconvenient that I would be extremely sad, which is *exactly* how I feel.

79

Observe Robert Walser's use of language to establish tone in *Jakob Von Gunten*:

> Recently I went with Schilinski to a top-class concert-café.
> How Schilinski trembled all over with timorousness. I behaved
> approximately like his kind father. The waiter ventured, after
> giving us a good look up and down, to ignore us; but when I
> requested him, with an enormously austere expression on my
> face, kindly to wait upon us, he at once became polite and
> brought us some light beer in tall, delicately cut goblets.

The reason people read books is so that they can feel intelligent and cultured, and Walser knows how to capitalize on this desire by crafting a literary environment that feels sophisticated. Notice the "concert-café" and "delicately cut goblets": details like this help build toward an overall mood of fanciness, which is like heroin to a reader of fiction. Include words like "timorousness" in your work and the reader's ego will be stroked, even if they don't know what it means.

Conversely, an author can exploit their audience's vanity by constructing a literary world filled with trashiness and buffoonery. To illustrate, let's look at this short passage from Denis Johnson's story "Emergency":

> Around 3:30 a.m. a guy with a knife in his eye came in, led by Georgie.

Now, instead of a snooty waiter or timorous, goblet-sipping Schilinski, we're presented with "a guy." No respectable person would still be awake at 3:30 in the morning, and the knife in the eye is entirely without class. Further, "Georgie" is an idiotic name, more suited for a pet guinea pig. While all of these choices come together to form a tone that couldn't be further from the fancy one observed in the Walser passage, the effect is the same. The reader will feel smart and sophisticated, by comparing themselves to these losers with dumb names who stay up too late.

80

Stream of consciousness is a literary technique where the writer attempts to capture the free-flowing ideas and emotions running through a character's head by writing in a loose, associative manner. William Faulkner made great use of this narrative mode in *The Sound and the Fury* and other works. Done successfully, stream of consciousness should resemble the thought processes of the human mind as it encounters or reflects on sensory information. To illustrate, I will improvise an example of stream of consciousness for you now:

The brook is babbling and winding through the town. A fire rages through the bread factory. Attention! Attention! The townspeople are nervous and spontaneously combust. Compost. Compose sentences. Molly is gone. I miss Molly. Giraffes extend their gorgeous necks. If I don't win Molly back I'll off myself with sleeping pills. Sleeping giants. Gigantism. I want to sleep with Molly or even just hold her. I need Molly to tell me everything will be all right. I hope her husband dies. The hippopotamus hops. The frog frogs. I'm going to call Molly from the pay phone in the subway station again and not say anything if she answers. I'm really falling apart here.

Point of View

81

Learning to see things from a variety of perspectives will help you write characters that have strong, believable motivations driving their actions. It's hard to see why a character would make the choices they make unless the author has a clear sense of what it might feel like to exist in that character's headspace. A recent incident tested my own ability to stand back and consider alternative vantage points. A few days ago, an email showed up in my inbox from Abe, the editor from Ballast Books. At first, I was elated. I'd just offered his son Patrick a 1999 First Edition Shadowless Holographic Charizard #4 if he helped me convince his father to publish *The Emerald*, and I assumed a book deal was about to materialize. Instead, Abe was furious. He'd discovered the direct messages between me and his son over Instagram. Although my username was Realpokemonfan1983, Abe figured out my true identity because of the many references to *The Emerald*. He said the whole thing was wildly inappropriate and creepy. Though he wouldn't be pursuing legal action this time, he warned me that if I ever contacted his son again, he would not hesitate to get the police involved. He recommended that I seek "professional help."

My initial reaction was confusion. It seemed like Abe was overreacting. Nobody had been hurt, and my plan was actually quite clever. But then I accessed my writer's brain and looked at the situation from his perspective: as far as he knew, I was actually a Pokémon card collector. He didn't know that I'd made all of that up in order to trick Patrick into helping me out with the manuscript. Abe assumed that I, a grown man, collected these silly cards for kids, and had parlayed this real interest into influencing his son. He must think I'm some kind of pedophile, I realized. Because what adult would collect Pokémon cards, unless they were utilizing this hobby in order to meet and seduce children? I thought about sending Abe an email clarifying that I didn't actually collect Pokémon cards and that I'd only feigned interest in them to get Patrick to help me with the manuscript, but he seems too angry to be reasoned with at the moment. Perhaps once he's had a chance to cool down, I'll explain to him that I'm not a child molester. Regardless, I think my chances of publishing *The Emerald* with Ballast Books have been destroyed. Which is actually fine—looking at their website now, it really seems like they're more focused on budget travel guides. *The Emerald* needs to come out with someone fully committed to publishing literary fiction, and Ballast just doesn't fit the bill. My debut novel coming out with Ballast Books would in fact signal the end of my writing career. It's funny how things work out perfectly sometimes.

82

Who is telling the story? The narrator's perspective plays an important role in fiction, so you want to have a solid handle on who they are and where they're coming from. A narrator who is prejudiced against Americans, for example, will process information differently from a narrator who isn't:

> Paul looked over as the door swung open. A filthy American walked into the room.

Or imagine if a story is told from the perspective of someone who is obsessed with food. The narrator's focus will always drift toward the snacks in the room. If there aren't any hot dogs or ice cream cones lying around, then this fatty will compare everything in the room to food items. Consider the influence of a food-obsessed narrator on the previous scene:

> Paul looked over as the door swung open. A huge donut rolled into the room.

Whether the narrator is an active participant in the story, or a detached observer delivering information to the reader, their inherent biases and judgements will affect how things unfold to varying degrees. A story could even be written from the perspective of someone from France:

Paul looked over as the door swung open. C'est la vie!

83

The narrator's perspective is often tied to the story's protagonist. This is obvious if you are writing in first-person, but third-person narration can also be privy to the main character's judgements. While the inner opinions and emotions of most of the story's characters are only suggested at through dialogue and visual clues, the narrator can directly access the protagonist's private feelings. This is incredibly useful when writing about undercover cops. When an undercover cop protagonist is dealing drugs or stealing a car, the narrator can remind the reader of this character's true intentions:

> Paul handed the gangster a briefcase filled with money. The gangster handed Paul a briefcase filled with cocaine. Paul didn't really want the cocaine, but buying it was part of his job. He was, after all, an undercover cop.

84

Many years ago, when I was still in university, I intervened in a mugging. I was strolling through High Park one afternoon, taking a break from my studies, when I heard a commotion coming from a nearby thicket. I pushed through the bushes and discovered an old woman being held at knifepoint by a man in a ski mask.

"I don't have anything else," the old woman whimpered. "Please, just leave me alone."

"Your jewellery," the man in the mask said. "Take it off."

"Hey!" I said.

The man turned around. He let go of the woman and started walking toward me. Knife held up in front of him—it was huge. A real, heavy-duty hunting knife.

"You got a problem, pal?" the man said. He kept moving toward me.

In the heat of the moment, I quickly removed my backpack. Two thick biology textbooks inside. I swung it back behind my head, and then hurled it right at the man's face. He ducked, and I ran straight toward him. Before he could stand back up and regain his footing, I lunged, and tackled him to the ground. He went down like a sack of meat. I quickly turned him over onto his chest and pinned his arms behind his back. The big knife was on the ground beside us. I kicked it away, into a bush.

"Go call the police," I said to the old woman. "There's a pay phone up the path a little, by the washrooms. I've got this guy under control. He's not going anywhere."

The cops eventually did come, and they commended me for my efforts. The man in the ski mask, it turned out, was an escaped convict who'd been in prison for murdering a cab driver years earlier. There was a nationwide manhunt for him. Who knows what the creep would've done if I hadn't happened upon him that day? I'm just happy he's off the streets.

The reason I'm bringing this up now is to make a point about first-person narration. This story, in fact, didn't actually happen to me. I never even went to university. Some guy named Tom O'Neil stumbled upon the mugging and then tackled the escaped convict. I read about it in the paper. It's a pretty impressive story, but when I tell people about it, I always say that *I* stopped the mugging. That *I* intervened. This is because if I said it happened to Tom O'Neil, nobody would really care. Who the hell is Tom O'Neil, they'd say. It's simply a better, more compelling story for my listener if I'm personally involved in the action. When I first told this story to Molly, her jaw dropped. I've related this mugging story to all the women I've been involved with over the years, usually on the first date. It's one of my go-to anecdotes at parties. I've even referenced it in a few wedding toasts.

People go crazy for it. That's because first-person narration feels more intimate and immediate, which is why you ought to always write your stories using the first-person "I." Nobody cares about some asshole named Tom O'Neil—they care about *you*, the storyteller.

85

A wonderful example of an author using first-person narration to build character can be found in Kazuo Ishiguro's *The Remains of the Day*, a novel about an English butler:

> The fact is, over the past few months, I have been responsible for a series of small errors in the carrying out of my duties. I should say that these errors have all been without exception quite trivial in themselves. Nevertheless, I think you will understand that to one not accustomed to committing such errors, this development was rather disturbing, and I did in fact begin to entertain all sorts of alarmist theories as to their cause.

Here we see how the author was able to take advantage of the first-person perspective to do a funny butler impression. If you have an amusing impression that you perform at parties, you can actually transpose this into an engaging narrative voice. The impression has to rely on the unique things a character might say, however, and not just a crazy-sounding voice. For example, many people have praised my spot-on Austin Powers impression, but to achieve the desired effect you need to actually hear me do the British accent. My Borat impression, however, could easily work on the page:

Hi, my name-a Borat. I like sex, it nice.

Just like with Ishiguro's butler, you get a strong sense of my Borat character's voice simply from reading the words in your head. Of course, I wouldn't call the character Borat. That would be plagiarism. I would name him Dildo.

86

Something you need to consider before beginning a new story is whether it will be written in the past or present tense. Past tense is more common. Writing in the past tense gives the action a sense of historical importance, like you're writing a record of significant events for future generations to consult. Present tense, while less common, is more effective at giving stories a feeling of urgency and so is probably the better option. To illustrate, imagine you're at a friend's house and they're giving you a tour. The property is quite old, and your friend tells you a story about how the original home had actually burned down, decades earlier. One of the previous owners had fallen asleep in bed while smoking, and their dropped cigarette started the blaze. Only the foundation remains; the rest has been completely reconstructed. Kind of an interesting story, right? Now imagine that this friend, instead, tells you there is a fire raging through the house *right now*. "My God!" your friend says. "The baby!" He runs upstairs. A flaming dog bursts into the room, igniting several pieces of furniture. Smoke everywhere. You're on the floor, coughing. You crawl toward the front door. A wooden beam falls on your spine, paralyzing you from the neck down. You use your jaw to propel yourself forward, inch-by-inch, while your shoes catch fire and begin to melt. And so on—you get the idea. Now, which story do you find more compelling? The one that happened a long time ago, to some old person you've never met? Or the story that's happening right here in the present tense, where you might actually die?

87

The tense you use in a story will obviously change the way the narrative is received by the reader, but it can also have an effect on the writer. When I began composing my Molly novel, I chose present tense. I found it comforting to write about the early days of our relationship as if I were living through those exhilarating moments again. Just by writing a sentence like "I lean in and kiss Molly," it really felt like I was leaning in and kissing Molly. I wrote a lot of sex scenes during this present-tense draft—this made me feel aroused, which helped relieve the stress of the breakup. I still consult these drafts now and then, when I'm feeling pent-up. But then I realized that writing in present-tense meant I was on a track that led straight to the scene where Molly and I split up, and I'd have to relive all of that pain again. Writing in past-tense, however, would allow me to remove this sensation of impending doom. I would tell the story from the perspective of a version of me that stood on the other side of the breakup, post-reconciliation, with our temporary separation existing as a brief narrative sequence that would only end up strengthening our relationship. Told from this point of view, the breakup chapters now feel like they capture a funny little story that Molly and I will eventually tell dinner guests, once we're back together: "We actually did break up for a short period. Remember that, honey? God, that was so silly. We must have been out of our minds." And now I'm realizing that this dinner party idea could be another interesting narrative device for the Molly novel. We're hosting a dinner party and I recount the whole story of the relationship to our guests. Molly chimes in now and again, but mainly it's me. We live on the Upper West Side of Manhattan at this point, and the dinner guests are esteemed New York artists and writers. Thomas Pynchon would be there, and Zadie Smith. Someone from *Saturday Night Live*–maybe Pete Davidson. And they're all listening with rapt attention as I play the raconteur. This will subconsciously make readers feel like they should also be captivated as they read through the novel, if they aren't captivated already, because these famous and smart dinner guests are clearly enthralled with my storytelling. In fact, a dumb guy could attend the dinner party too, and he's the only one who is bored by the story. He's not famous or anything. I could show him yawning and constantly checking his phone. Then if a reader happens to find themselves bored by the novel, they'll be identifying with the dumb guy at the table, instead of Zadie Smith and so on. Maybe former US president Barack Obama is there too. He asks me to sign his copy of *The Emerald*. I write: "Thanks for all your support, Barry. Enjoy!"

88

Future tense is not something you see employed in works of fiction too often. With future tense, the narrator informs the reader about events that will eventually and inevitably unfold. Instead of "Paul rode the bus to work," we learn that "Paul shall ride the bus to work." Future tense sounds ominous—almost like a psychic is telling the story as they gaze into their crystal ball, which would be a fantastic narrative device. An entire novel could be written from the perspective of a fortune teller looking into their crystal ball. Now that I've documented the idea here, I have claimed legal ownership of this intellectual property so nobody can steal it. Perhaps the novel about my relationship with Molly could be written like this. As if I went to a carnival as a child, and I walked into a tent and met this old, gnarled woman wearing tons of jewellery, and she's a psychic, and I ask her if I'll ever fall in love. Then the whole Molly novel is this psychic telling kid-me about the relationship I'll have with Molly as an adult. At the end of the novel, I walk out of the old lady's carnival tent and say, "Gee, that was a waste of five bucks.

What a lunatic!" But then I see something that the psychic told me I'd see, like a red bird or something. I run back to the psychic's tent, but it's gone. I see one of her rings lying in the dirt. That's it. That's my ending.

89

A story's narrator can take on the voice and personality of one of the characters. This is called free indirect style. Even though free indirect style is written in third-person, the narrator incorporates the protagonist's unique traits and quirks the way a first-person narrator might. Here is a scene written with normal third-person narration:

> The cowboy stood waiting in the checkout line. He sighed, realizing he would be late for work again.

Now here is that same scene, written using the free indirect style:

> The cowboy stood waiting in the darn tootin' checkout line. He sighed, realizing he would be late for rootin' tootin' work again.

90

Usually, you want to avoid using second-person narration. This is because people don't like being told what to do. Let's say you start a story with this sentence: "You take the bus to the zoo." Unless your reader is actually planning on taking the bus to the zoo, their first thought is going to be something like, "No, I don't. I don't like the zoo. Even if I did like it, I certainly wouldn't take the bus there." And now you've lost them. If you really want to write in second-person, however, there is a way to make it work: right at the beginning of your story, have an authority figure give your protagonist orders and then show your protagonist refusing to comply. By witnessing the second-person protagonist defy an authority's commands, the reader will be tricked into identifying with your protagonist's apparent freedom and now allow you, the author, to order them around within the story. Here's an example of how to successfully begin a story using second-person narration:

You answer the door. It's the chief of police.

"I need you to come with me to the station," the chief of police says. "That's an order!"

"Nah," you say. You slam the door in the chief's face.

You sit back down on the couch and pick up the Xbox controller. Instead of going to the police station, you play Xbox and eat snacks all day.

91

It can be beneficial, not just with writing fiction, but in life, to try and view situations from multiple perspectives. If you get caught up in a disagreement with someone, step back and really consider where they're coming from. This can help you find common ground and diffuse potentially volatile encounters. It can also train you to inhabit a variety of perspectives in your writing, which is an invaluable skill to have.

When I first learned how miserable Molly's husband Charles had become since they'd separated, and saw that he watched old home movies of him and Molly, crying like a petulant child, I felt guilty. Maybe he deserved another chance. He and Molly had been married for decades. Sure, Molly was a grown woman and had made her choice, but what if they only needed some time apart to take stock and repair things? But then I learned that Charles was actively campaigning for her to take him back, by reaching out to their mutual friends and organizing a concerted effort to bully Molly into salvaging the marriage. Calls came in at all hours, along with drop-ins from friends and family members who wanted to "check in." Often I would be there, in Molly's apartment, and had to hide in the bedroom while Molly endured these intrusions. It was harassment, really. All of it orchestrated by Charles. That's when I realized I'd been looking at things through a single, narrow perspective—Charles's. I hadn't considered the circumstances from my own perspective. Molly made me happy, and I was making her happy, too. Charles was the real threat. A threat that needed to be neutralized. I knew I had to convince Molly to procure an official divorce and then commit to me.

I got to work immediately. I employed a two-pronged attack: one was subconscious, where I would leave pro-divorce literature that I'd printed from the internet lying around Molly's apartment, or tell her stories about made-up friends who incidentally had gone through divorces and were now much, much happier. The other prong was more direct, where I would take Molly to Albert's and use their crayons to scrawl giant pros and cons lists on the tablecloth. In the cons section, I would write down everything that was toxic and wrong with Charles. In the pros list, I would lay out my many attributes, which underscored how continuing our relationship would be beneficial to Molly. "I'm not leaving you," Molly would say. "You don't need to do all this." But I knew the only way to ensure Charles's defeat would be to take an active role in destroying him. And I did destroy him. Molly served him divorce papers within the month. He was devastated. I watched him through his living room window the day he was served, moaning on the couch like a dying, pregnant cat. I wrote "I WIN" backwards on the window with my finger, where my breath had fogged up the glass. I hope he saw it. And if he thinks he can win Molly back now that she's left me, he can think again. Regardless, it's interesting that all of this was possible because I stepped outside of Charles's perspective and looked at the situation from another viewpoint—my own.

92

An interesting technique to experiment with is employing an unreliable narrator. This is when you have the narrator lie to the reader. For example, your narrator might say a certain character is going to go to the beach. Now that the reader expects this character to go to the beach, have them not go to the beach. Have them go somewhere else. Or have them stay where they are, away from the beach. The reader won't expect this, and so you're keeping them on their toes. It's a good trick to use when you start running out of ideas.

93

Sometimes an unreliable narrator can call into question the reliability of the author. To illustrate, here is a scene from Kingsley Amis's *Lucky Jim*:

> A dusty thudding in his head made the scene before him beat like a pulse. His mouth had been used as a latrine by some small creature of the night, and then as its mausoleum. During the night, too, he'd somehow been on a cross-country run and then been expertly beaten up by secret police.

This is quite a tale, but we know from the previous chapter that the narrator is lying: there were no small creatures or secret police; the protagonist never went on any cross-country runs. In fact, the protagonist had been drinking alcohol all night. So why lie now? Or did the narrator lie earlier about the drinking? The most likely scenario is that the author forgot what he'd written in the previous chapter and threw in this ridiculous stuff about the mausoleum and secret police on a whim, unaware that he was contradicting himself. Amis himself was probably drunk at the time, and somehow this egregious error slipped by the editor. Maybe the editor was drunk too. *Lucky Jim* came out in 1954—*every*body was drunk back then.

94

It's been an interesting exercise to supplement my writing income with full-time work at Value Village, because I can now truly understand the perspective of someone who would actually work at Value Village full-time. Even though I'm a professional writer, by going in every day and performing the tasks that someone employed by Value Village would perform, I get to experience what life is like for a real, paycheck-to-paycheck, working stiff, and this feeds into my creative life. That's why it doesn't bother me when, say, the manager ridicules me in front of the customers for being "the slowest cashier he's ever seen," which is debatable. Because that's what it's really like for working-class grunts. At staff meetings, their managers say things like "So when's your book coming out, huh? When you buy a new ink cartridge for your printer?" This kind of comment doesn't upset me at all, because I get to see, first-hand, what life is like for the common folk. They have these mean managers. This insight allows me to write believable working-class characters, even though my real job is to be a writer and Value Village is only a temporary side thing.

95

While empathy is an important quality for a fiction writer to have, you don't want to be *too* empathetic. This happens when an author overreaches and tries to convey an irrational character's perspective as if logic and reason were at work. Sometimes people are just crazy. I'm reminded of when Molly, early in our relationship, expressed her worries over my uncle Herman. "Has he been to see a mental health professional?" she said. "He needs help. I think he's really suffering." Of course, Molly's concern was definitely cute and this hopeful attitude is part of her charm, but what she didn't understand is that Uncle Herman's always been that way. He's a nutty guy. That's just Uncle Herman being Uncle Herman.

96

If you're having trouble writing from a point of view different from your own, it can be helpful to play-act as someone else. Go out into the world and pretend to be another person. Test out a new personality on a barista or the stranger sitting next to you on the bus. Think of a backstory and draw from it during these interactions. As you get more practice, your improvisational skills will improve and you'll be able to more fully inhabit these new characters. That's how I came up with my character Billy the Dog Catcher, the protagonist of a short story I recently sent to *The New Yorker*. I was at Molly's ex-husband's house months ago, gathering intel, when I tripped over a rock in the garden. I guess I yelped, which alerted Charles, who came running outside and found me lying in the lilies beneath his living room window. He helped me up, then asked me who I was and what I was doing in his yard. In the heat of the moment, I blurted out that I was Billy. I used a southern accent, like a Louisiana drawl. I said I was a dog catcher looking for a loose dog, y'all. He said he didn't realize that "dog catcher" was a real job, and that he'd only ever seen them in comic strips. He asked me where my dog-catching equipment was. I stammered for a minute, then told him dog-catching was definitely real, and actually a growing industry, and that it wasn't like in the cartoons. We didn't carry around giant nets and whatnot. We just grab them with our hands, which helps keep the business cost-effective. He asked me what kind of dog I was looking for, and I froze up. I couldn't think of any dog breeds. I eventually said "normal dog," and Charles seemed suspicious. But then I amended my answer: "Labrador, y'all." I excused myself, and Charles was none the wiser. Not only had I fooled him, but I'd created a new character with a deep backstory and compelling accent.

97

One interesting approach to consider is writing an epistolary novel. An epistolary novel is written as a series of documents. Things like letters, diary entries, newspaper clippings, and emails are juxtaposed together to tell a unified story. You can actually turn your already completed novel into an epistolary novel in order to jazz it up, if publishers seem uninterested. If the story is written in first-person, simply add "Dear Diary" before each chapter. If it's written in third-person, you need to turn the chapters into newspaper articles. To do this, simply add headlines which sum up what happens in each chapter in a newspapery manner, and then include the geographic location for extra authenticity. To illustrate, let's first look at the opening lines of Don DeLillo's *Libra*:

> This was the year he rode the subway to the ends of the city, two hundred miles of track. He liked to stand at the front of the first car, hands against the glass. The train smashed through the dark. People stood on local platforms staring nowhere, a look they'd been practising for years.

This is perfectly fine, but now imagine a world where the author had decided to put in a little more effort here and spice things up, epistolary-style:

MAN RIDES SUBWAY FOR ONE YEAR

NEW YORK CITY—This was the year he rode the subway to the ends of the city, two hundred miles of track. He liked to stand at the front of the first car, hands against the glass. The train smashed through the dark. People stood on local platforms staring nowhere, a look they'd been practising for years.

Oh, what could have been!

Dialogue

98

When writing dialogue, try and capture the real way people talk. We don't always use complete sentences or express ourselves in a perfectly logical, clear manner. We don't dole out neat little packages of exposition with everything we say. We contradict ourselves. We ignore the other speaker. We lie and use slang and misspeak. Let's look at a scene from F. Scott Fitzgerald's *The Great Gatsby*:

> I told her how I had stopped off in Chicago for a day on my way East, and how a dozen people had sent their love through me.
>
> "Do they miss me?" she cried ecstatically.
>
> "The whole town is desolate. All the cars have the left rear wheel painted black as a mourning wreath, and there's a persistent wail all night along the north shore."
>
> "How gorgeous! Let's go back, Tom. Tomorrow!" Then she added irrelevantly: "You ought to see the baby."
>
> "I'd like to."
>
> "She's asleep. She's three years old. Haven't you ever seen her?"
>
> "Never."

While *The Great Gatsby* has many merits and is an undeniable classic, the dialogue leaves something to be desired. People don't actually talk the way the characters in the previous scene do. It sounds much too *written*. Let's look at the scene again, edited by me to reflect the way in which real humans engage in conversation:

> I told her how I had stopped off in Chicago for a day on my way East, and how a dozen people had sent their love through me.
>
> "Sup, bitch?" she cried ecstatically.
>
> "Meh."
>
> "I'm horny as hell." Then she added irrelevantly: "You ought to see the baby."
>
> "Natch."
>
> "She's a lil' bitch."
>
> "Meh."

99

While you should aim for verisimilitude with your dialogue, sometimes the way in which people speak in the real world can feel flat and oddly phoney on the page. For instance, I recently wrote the scene for my Molly novel where Molly informs me that she wants to stop keeping our relationship a secret. After finally setting her divorce in motion, she thought it was time to let her friends and family know about us, and she called to tell me this while I was working on an important story submission (to *The New Yorker*). At first, I urged caution—what if everyone ganged up on her and told her she was making a mistake? What if my mother started intruding and everyone else began chiming in too, which could spoil the romance and all the fun we were having by keeping things private? But Molly insisted, and I relented. "Fine," I said, and hung up. Molly kept calling, but I was busy with my submission and so put my phone on silent. Once I submitted my story, I called her back and explained how I was swamped with writing duties (another story submission to *The New Yorker*). She was worried that I was angry with her and I had to explain, again, that I was simply busy. "Writing is my job,"

I said. "You wouldn't interrupt me like this if I was performing spinal surgery, would you?" She went on to say that she was nervous about telling her sisters about us, and wanted to talk things through with me first. I told her that this was a sign she ought to wait, but she insisted that this was something she needed to do right away. "Then just tell them already!" I said. "What are you bothering me about it for?" I hung up on her. Again, if this seems rude on my part, remember that writing is a real job and I was busy working. Submitting stories to *The New Yorker* is a writer's version of spinal surgery. But anyway, the point is that when I attempted to capture this important moment—when our relationship "went public"—in my novel, the whole thing felt sort of fake. It just didn't have that snappy, real, literary energy that good dialogue should have. Then I tried rewriting the scene with dialogue which, though entirely fictional, felt much more realistic. Now, in the novel, I wasn't busy with my *New Yorker* submission and was instead able to be more supportive and encouraging of Molly as she made this difficult step. Because even though *New Yorker* submissions are like spinal surgery for a working writer, my character came across as a bit cold and uncaring in the initial draft, which obviously does not reflect the reality of the situation. Would you call a surgeon cold and uncaring if he told his girlfriend to stop calling him while he was in the middle of a spinal surgery? No, you wouldn't. The patient could die if the surgeon became distracted, which would be insane.

100

Everyone has their own agenda. Always keep in mind that every character in your story is on their own journey, and has their own goals. When writing dialogue, it's important to remember that your characters shouldn't only be saying things that help move your protagonist's story forward—the supporting characters have their own stories which they should be attempting to advance through the things they say. Here's an example of dialogue where both characters are only interested in furthering the main character's plot:

> "Can I borrow your dirt bike?" Paul said. "I need to go rescue my best friend."
> "Yes!" Nancy said.

Now what if the supporting character, Nancy, were to have her own personal plans? This will make the dialogue feel more authentic and give Nancy agency:

"Can I borrow your dirt bike?" Paul said. "I need to go rescue my best friend."

"I'll lend it to you," Nancy said. "But first you have to give me $200 so I can pay off Jimmy Hoffa."

101

You can use dialogue to show off your character's skills and abilities. Here's a scene from James Salter's *A Sport and a Pastime*:

> He knew how to handle her. He's the only man who knows how to make her feel like a woman.
> "Isn't that right, sweetheart?" she says.
> "That's right, Bummy."

Here, the protagonist claims he can "handle" this woman and make her feel like a woman. But is the reader just supposed to take his word for it? That's why Salter shows us, through dialogue, how adept his protagonist really is when it comes to relationships. The protagonist calls the woman "Bummy," and so we are able to see his women-handling skills at work. He knows *exactly* what to say to make her feel like a woman: "That's right, Bummy." Perfect.

102

Attributives are used to signal who the speaker is when presenting a line of dialogue. The most common type of attributive is "she said" or "Paul said," etc. Using "said" over and over again gets old fast, however, so you want to replace most of these with fun verbs. For strong, masculine characters you can use verbs associated with dangerous animals, like bears: Paul growled, snarled, barked, and roared. For female characters and spineless men, use verbs associated with birds: Paul chirped, squawked, tweeted, and cooed.

You can also use a beat instead of an attributive. A beat is when you include a character's action next to a piece of dialogue to signal who is speaking. This can be an efficient way to take care of necessary business during dialogue-heavy passages. If your character smokes, dialogue beats can be a great opportunity for them to enjoy cigarettes, without having to waste space by including all these long smoking scenes. Beats can also be used for product placements, if you're fortunate enough to have a sponsored content deal:

"Paul, I want a divorce." Nancy cracked open an ice-cold can of Sprite.

"What about our daughter?" Paul eyed Nancy's Sprite and licked his lips. He reached into the mini-fridge and pulled out a Sprite of his own.

"She'll get over it." Nancy took a long, delicious sip of Sprite. "And by the way, she's living with me."

"Can I at least see her on weekends?" Paul sipped his Sprite and smiled.

"Absolutely not!" Nancy took another sip of Sprite and thought about how delicious it tasted.

103

Sometimes beats can be used to show the subtext of a conversation. If a character says things that conflict with how they actually feel, the reader can be clued into this interesting dynamic through the character's actions during the conversation. I had to write a scene like this for the Molly novel, actually. It was a dialogue-heavy sequence that takes place after Molly told her friends and family about our relationship. Molly called me up to tell me how these first few conversations went. She'd talked to both her sisters, as well as her old friend Louise, and the reactions were pretty critical. They all thought she was moving too fast into a new relationship and that she ought to wait on the divorce. Maybe things with Charles could still be repaired, they cautioned. Molly made it clear to them that she was firm in her decision, however. Still, the lack of support and understanding from her sisters and Louise had upset her, and Molly needed my reassurance. I told her that everything was going to be fine. Her sisters and friends would come around eventually. I reminded her of how good things were with us and how the divorce was such a smart move.

Inside, however, I was panicking. Maybe Molly's sisters were right, I thought. This was all a big mistake. We were having fun, sure, but Molly and her husband had been together for so long. They'd been through so much. They had a son together, and then watched him die in the hospital. And the age difference, my God. We were from different worlds. We wouldn't last. But of course I couldn't say any of these things to Molly. She needed to be comforted, and I was only having a momentary freak out.

One way to write this scene would be to interrupt the conversation with my character's thoughts, so that the reader could see what was really going on in my head at the time. The more interesting approach, however, would be to use dialogue beats that suggest my interior state. I came up with the idea to have my character mowing the lawn during this phone call with Molly (in real life, I was sitting on my couch, watching television). And so, with each beat that attributed a line of dialogue to my character, I would refer to myself pushing the mower, kicking a large rock out of the mower's path, wiping sweat from my brow, etc. Then, after Molly and I finish talking, I hang up the phone and turn off the mower. I stand back, assess my completed yard work, and realize that I'd unknowingly mowed the words "I MADE A BIG MISTAKE" into the lawn. The subtext of the conversation is now made clear, and I was able to deliver it in an interesting, subtle manner.

It's a powerful scene, but its inclusion presented a few problems. First, I'd already established that I lived in an apartment building with my uncle Herman, so what lawn was I mowing?

This was an easy fix: I used the find and replace tool in Microsoft Word to change all instances of "apartment" and "building" into the word "house." Easy. The other issue with the scene was that lawn mowers are notoriously loud machines, so how was my character able to talk with Molly while simultaneously mowing the lawn? Why wouldn't I just turn off the mower until I was done with the phone call? Fixing this problem took a bit more work: I went back to an earlier chapter and established that a product called the Lawn Mower Silencer existed through a radio ad that my character overhears. According to the ad, the Lawn Mower Silencer attaches to your mower and muffles the noise, so you can mow quietly. "I should get that for my lawn mower," my character says. Then I wrote in a quick shopping scene a few chapters later, where I purchase the Lawn Mower Silencer. Then another quick scene where I attach the Lawn Mower Silencer to my lawn mower. And so now, when readers get to the part where Molly calls me and I talk to her while mowing the lawn, it will all make sense.

104

Occasionally, an author will get rid of attributives and beats altogether. In Cormac McCarthy's *The Road*, even quotation marks are ignored when delivering dialogue:

> Are we going to die?
>> Sometime. Not now.
>> And we're still going south.
>> Yes.
>> So we'll be warm.
>> Yes.

While McCarthy's dialogue might seem confusing—who is speaking? Is this a character talking, or the narrator narrating?—the author is able to project an air of nonchalance. It feels like he slapped things together quickly, not bothering to use quotations, and didn't even hire an editor. It's like McCarthy is saying, "Oh, this story? I just kind of jotted it down when I was bored. I wasn't even trying, really. It's whatever." And because McCarthy acts as if minimal effort goes into writing his novels, critics always go easy on him. This can be an effective technique if you're insecure and want to pre-empt any complaints readers might have about your work.

105

With dialogue, you're allowed to make mistakes and spell things however you like. The copy editor is powerless when it comes to dialogue, so this is where you can really express your freedom as an artist. Here's a line from Zadie Smith's novel *Swing Time*:

"Cyan do nuttin wid er. Always been like dat."

Is there a reason why Smith spelled these words in this unusual way? Not at all. The author simply knew she could get away with funny spellings because it's part of the dialogue, which is a kind of hall pass for writers who want to "get weird."

106

Dialogue doesn't always have to forward the plot, reveal important information about a character, or deliver some kind of meaningful symbolic message. It can just *be*. Take a look at this scene from Nicholson Baker's *Vox*:

> "What are you wearing under your shirt?"
> "A bra."
> "What kind of bra?"
> "A nothing bra. A normal, white bra bra."
> "Oooo!"

Here we see that one of the characters is turned on, and probably wants to have sex. Although the phrase "Oooo!" is meaningless on its own, through context we can infer that the speaker is expressing how turned on they are by what the other person just said. Baker's efficient use of dialogue also rings true to life: if you were really turned on and wanted to have sex with someone, you wouldn't say "I'm really turned on and want to have sex with you." You'd say "Oooo!"

107

Take a look at the opening line of John Cheever's short story "The Swimmer":

> It was one of those midsummer Sundays when everyone sits around saying, "I *drank* too much last night."

Cheever is demonstrating an interesting technique here, where instead of presenting us with a long, tedious scene where everyone says the exact same thing, over and over, he summarizes all this with one efficient line of dialogue. While uncommon, you may find yourself at a place in your story where a large crowd of people takes turns repeating the same phrase. Perhaps you're writing about a cult where the members chant little slogans to each other. Capturing all of this in detail might help you fill up a few pages if you're anxious to finish, but will inevitably bore the reader. Instead, like Cheever, you need to summarize. Here's what "The Swimmer" might look like if Cheever instead chose to present the scene as it happened:

> It was one of those midsummer Sundays when everyone sits around. "I *drank* too much last night," the swimmer said.

"I *drank* too much last night," another guy said.

"I *drank* too much last night," the swimmer's mom said.

"I *drank* too much last night," an old guy said.

"I *drank* too much last night," the old guy's friend said.

"I *drank* too much last night," the chief of police said.

"I *drank* too much last night," a different old guy said.

108

Sometimes the things people *don't* say can be as important, or even more important, than the things they do say. One evening, around the time that Molly served Charles divorce papers and told her friends and family about our relationship, she called me up in distress. I saw her name light up my phone, but I didn't answer. She left a voice mail:

> I hope you're okay. I'm having a hard time here. Just got off the phone with Louise. She thinks I'm acting crazy and I know I'm not, but it's frustrating. Why can't everyone see how much better things are for me now? Maybe they need to meet you and see how amazing you are. I don't know. But I feel so alone right now. Do you think you could come over tonight, Sam? Or I could come over there? I don't want to be alone. Please call me back when you get this, dear.

My response to this emotional plea? There was none. I listened to the voice mail, then put my phone on silent. I remember I was feeling really tired. If I'm being honest, I was starting to find Molly's neediness around this time a little annoying. I just wanted a night to relax, by myself, without Molly's constant appeals for reassurance. I remember it was a Saturday and I wanted to watch *Saturday Night Live*, even though it was an off-week and they were showing a rerun. I'm actually a little ashamed of this now. I should have at least called her back. I've been debating about whether to include this scene in the novel, but I now think that I should. Show my true self. Many of you reading this might think of me as this almighty, faultless man, because I've written all of these great works, but the truth is that I'm not perfect. Far from it. Just because I write great books, it doesn't mean that I always make great decisions. In fact, part of what makes brilliant writers so brilliant is that they've learned to be humble. Don't place me on a pedestal—I'm right here on the dusty old floor with the rest of you. Maybe that's what makes my work so relatable.

109

With dialogue, you can use regional dialects to signal to the reader where the character is from. Here's a scene from Graham Greene's *Brighton Rock*:

"Have a drink?"
    "Thanks. I'll have a gin."
    "Cheeryo."
    "Cheeryo."

We can tell that the two speakers are English, because of the use of "cheeryo," an expression popular with the Brits. If you want to show that a character is American, you can similarly use an American expression like "howdy" or "eat my shorts." Australian characters will say "mate." Jamaican characters say "mon." Italian characters say "mamma mia." If a character is from France or some other country where they don't speak English, either have them speak their native language or show them fumbling around with English, which can be hilarious. Someone who lives in an isolated, rural area where they get a lot of storms might have a pronounced stutter, due to being struck by lightning. If your character is in hiding—an Anne Frank type—you can make the font a bit smaller to show that they are whispering. You can also use the small-font trick for characters from developing countries, because it shows that they're weak from starvation.

110

Discussions between characters are not the only source of dialogue; characters can also have internal conversations. Thoughts in fiction function just like dialogue, except the other characters in the scene obviously aren't privy to this information. This can be useful, especially if you've established that your protagonist is polite and abides by social conventions. When they encounter an obvious freak or loser, your well-mannered protagonist won't be able to express an amusing observation about this person without sacrificing reader sympathy. For example, if your main character meets a man with a large waistline and calls them a tub of lard, the reader will turn against your protagonist. If the protagonist just thinks to themselves "get a load of this tub of lard," however, the reader will only laugh and continue with their support. Or let's say your main character comes across a guy in a wheelchair. Obviously, they need to make some sort of funny comment, but doing so out loud will make your protagonist seem like a monster. Instead, have them think of the funny comment and then choose to not say it. Now your protagonist will actually seem kind and considerate.

111

An exercise you can use to improve your dialogue-capturing skills is to surreptitiously record audio of people out in the world, and then transcribe what you hear on the recording. This will help you learn to mimic the way people actually converse with each other, and it will give you a chance to practise translating human speech into literary prose. Here's a transcription of a recent recording I made with my phone, at a café near my building:

> "I honestly don't even care if he calls me back at this point. I'm over—"
>> "Oh my God, do you smell something?"
>> "Ugh, yes. What is that?"
>> "Oh, it might be that guy at the next table."
>> "What?"
>> "Shh. Nothing, never mind."
>> "What guy?"
>> "Never mind. Lower your voice. Let's just move to that table over there."

This exchange is of particular interest because I was right there next to these two women, and I didn't smell anything unusual. Which means that the one woman who first pointed out the smell is crazy, and that the other woman is a liar for going along with the first woman's fantasy. Such an interesting dynamic, which I was able to glean from only a few lines of dialogue.

Meaning

112

What is the point of fiction? What does it all *mean*? How can a story move beyond simple entertainment and provide us with something deeper and more profound? One surefire way to create meaningful work is to use your stories to point out that certain things in society are problematic. And while an editorial essay will explicitly state which thing in society is problematic, fiction can be more ambiguous, leaving the reader to figure out exactly what real-world problematic thing the story is referring to. For example, a novelist might write about a mean and tyrannical politician who ruins everything but then receives their comeuppance in the end. The reader can determine for themselves which political figure or party the character is supposed to represent, depending on the reader's own personal opinions. Because of this, the novel now can appeal to everyone, unlike narrow-minded editorialists who must confine themselves to a rigid world view and alienate half of their readership. A good novelist should take hard, uncompromising stances on issues, which can then be interpreted in any number of ways by a wide and diverse audience. Now every reader will have a deep, impactful experience, and nobody will have to feel uncomfortable.

113

Upon waking from an interesting dream, you can consult a dream dictionary and look up the things you saw in the dream to determine the dream's meaning. If an abacus appears in your dream, it means that you have out-of-date views. That's just an example I found on the first page of my dream dictionary—I have wonderfully progressive views and have never dreamt about an abacus myself. But the interesting thing about fiction is that you can actually reverse-engineer symbolic meaning into your work by using a dream dictionary to figure out what images and items need to appear in the story. If one of your characters has out-of-date views, you can show them operating an abacus. Or you could even change their name to Abacus. The average, uneducated person might not notice details like this, but more intellectual readers who own dream dictionaries will appreciate the clever use of symbolism.

114

Sometimes the deeper meaning of a story won't be apparent from the outset. A writer may compose a story, paying close attention to the plot and characters without any real sense of *why* they're writing this particular story. Later on, perhaps even upon completion of the story, the narrative's themes will reveal themselves to the author. I'm currently working on a section in my Molly novel where the protagonist goes out of his way to avoid his elderly girlfriend in her time of need. After Molly filed for a divorce and told everyone that she was seeing someone else, the reactions from her friends and family ranged from skeptical to incredulous. She was feeling alone and vulnerable, but I distanced myself from her. I rarely answered her calls. When I did answer, my tone was often quite cold. When she asked me to meet up, I'd say I was too busy. And I *was* busy with my writing—I always am—but I could have carved out some time for Molly. During this uncomfortable period, I did see Molly on a couple of occasions, and we even had sex in her bed, but there was a new awkwardness between us. Molly didn't understand why my attitude toward her had changed so suddenly, and I kept denying that it had changed.

But it had. And I'm not sure why, exactly, either. I guess I was overwhelmed. But this seems like an important section of my novel, and I'm having a difficult time writing about it. Why was I acting this way toward Molly? And why am I writing about it now? Who wants to read a book about this bumbling idiot who convinces his girlfriend to divorce her husband and then hides away from her? Why do I bother to write at all? No one will publish me. I flamed out with Abe and Ballast Books, which was probably my best shot. *The Emerald* is a failure, and the Molly novel will fail too. So much time wasted, when I could have been doing something productive. I could have been volunteering at a food bank. Anything else, really. All I know is that life is hard. If there is a god, they are a vindictive and harsh god. We're all just struggling along as things get worse and worse. And everything we do is pointless.

I recognize that I'm being overdramatic, and I'm actually half-joking about some of this stuff. The point I'm trying to make is that even though this section of the Molly novel—and the Molly novel project overall—may seem like meaningless drivel at the moment, later on its deeper thematic importance will reveal itself to me. I just need to push through and trust in the process. Life isn't all that hard. It only seems that way sometimes. Of course *The Emerald* will get published. The Molly novel, too. These books will likely do quite well, both critically and financially. The stuff about everything being pointless was obviously a little joke. Things aren't getting worse for me. In fact, everything is fine.

115

There's an important tool which writers need to master if they want to connect with an audience: pathos. This is when a work appeals to the emotions of the reader and elicits feelings which already reside within them. A common example of pathos at work are those TV commercials for charities which showcase starving Third World children or disfigured pets. By drawing on the emotions of the audience, these commercials are able to persuade viewers to either donate money to help starving Third World children, or adopt disfigured pets. With fiction, you can create pathos in your work using this same strategy: make all of your characters starving Third Word children and disfigured pets. In turn, your readers will "donate" their money to buy your next book. They will also "adopt" your next book, by purchasing it.

116

A note on authenticity: people aren't perfect. They have flaws and quirks, and the characters in your fiction ought to reflect this reality. Give your protagonist diabetes, as well as a lisp. A limp could work well too. There should be stains on their shirt. Poor hygiene. Make them xenophobic. Their apartment should be messy—all of your characters should be hoarders with serious mental disabilities. Or put them in a prison. For murder, or trying to blow up a hospital. They should be disliked by all the other inmates. They should have long, gross arms. *That*'s what real people are like.

117

A story's theme is not the same as the story's subject. The theme is the main idea *behind* a story. For example, the subject of a novel could be war, and the novel's theme is that war is bad. Another story might have "murder mystery" as its subject, while the theme of the story is that murdering people is bad. The easiest way to establish a powerful theme is to write about something that is clearly bad, like war or murdering people, and then the story's theme can be pointing out how it's bad.

118

Bringing humour into your story can actually add great depth and diversity to the narrative. Perhaps you've written a sombre scene, with two depressed characters discussing a sad turn of events in a rainy parking lot. Scenes like this can be a slog for the reader. Take a look at this excerpt from Per Petterson's *Out Stealing Horses*:

> "Bloody hell," I said.
>
> "I was just eighteen," he said. "It's long ago, but I shall never forget it."
>
> "Then I can well understand why you will never shoot a dog again."

What an absolute downer. Who in their right mind wants to listen to these two buzzkills discuss shooting a dog? If the writer were to inject humour into the passage, however, the grim tone would be leavened with joy, and the reader might stick around a bit longer. A simple, effective method for adding humour to a piece of writing is to introduce an old, senile man who sits in the corner of the room and shouts random words. Let's look at

Petterson's example again, this time revised by me to include some much-needed comic relief:

"Bloody hell," I said.

"I was just eighteen," he said. "It's long ago, but I shall never forget it."

"Computer program!" the old, senile man in the corner shouted.

"Then I can well understand why you will never shoot a dog again."

"Buttholes!"

119

I'd written a scene for my Molly novel that felt rather dour and needlessly slowed down the pace of the book. In the scene (and in real life), I'd taken Molly out for lasagna at Albert's to celebrate her divorce. We hadn't seen each other for a few weeks, and Molly was worried that I was losing interest in her. I told her that she was talking nonsense and to just relax. We weren't saying much. Molly seemed on the verge of tears and the whole thing was rather uncomfortable. And then, by chance, a local author I know walked into the restaurant—we'll call him James. James had published a few books of poetry with small presses and hosted a monthly reading series, which I had attended. I'd been angling to read at one of these events, but wanted to secure a publishing deal for *The Emerald* first, which would lend my debut performance an air of literary legitimacy and allow me to possibly headline the evening. Anyway, when James walked into Albert's with his wife, he spotted me instantly, came over to say hello, and I panicked. While Molly had informed her friends and family of our relationship, I hadn't told a soul. Uncle Herman didn't know. Molly's friends in the book club likely told my mother, but I'd been ducking her calls. And so when James came up to our table, I introduced Molly as my cleaning lady. I said I had a tradition where I treated "my staff" to a one-on-one meal on their birthdays. "Oh, isn't that nice," James said. "Nice to meet you, Molly, and happy birthday!" When he walked away, Molly started crying into her napkin. We finished the meal in silence.

I'd written this scene into the book as it happened, and obviously it landed with a thud. Much too depressing. You want to always give the reader at least a glimmer of light to guide them through your stories, or else they'll abandon you. I thought about how I might add some humour to the scene, thereby lightening the mood, and the cleaning lady thing made me think of *Mrs. Doubtfire*. Such a funny movie: if you haven't seen it, Robin Williams plays a divorced man who dresses up as a female housekeeper so he can see his kids. This gave me the idea of having Molly and I decide to swap clothes when James entered the restaurant. "Quick, meet me in the washroom," my character says to Molly. "I'm not ready to go public with our relationship yet, and so we need to switch outfits." Molly rolls her eyes but complies. Then I come out of the bathroom wearing Molly's dress and shoes and pearl necklace. My makeup done up to look just like Molly's. Molly's in my jeans and Penguin Random House T-shirt. There's this funny interaction where our server is confused, and we try to convince him that we'd only traded seats. Then one of the crusty buns I'd stuffed Molly's bra with falls out and rolls across the floor. Meanwhile, James doesn't recognize me at all, and Molly and I finish our meal in peace. The restaurant scene, bolstered with comedic elements, now struck the right tone.

But then I thought about really taking advantage of the amusing set-up. I added in that James glances over at our table, notices me wearing Molly's clothes, and starts giving me these looks. He doesn't recognize me. Instead, he thinks I'm this beautiful woman; so beautiful, in fact, he's willing to risk flirting with me while eating dinner with his wife. He keeps blowing me kisses and then, when Molly goes to the washroom, he comes over and whispers his phone number into my ear. "Call me later," James says. "I'll get us a motel room. This is so crazy." And now I'm wondering if this restaurant scene could come at the beginning of the novel and kick off what could actually be a fun, farcical romp, à la *Mrs. Doubtfire*. I'm thinking it might even work better as a screenplay. Get the Farrelly Brothers involved. Forget *The New Yorker*—Hollywood is where the real interesting work is being done these days.

120

Metaphors can be used to add context, illustrate an idea, describe a scene more accurately, or draw meaningful comparisons between different elements. Essentially, a metaphor is when you say that a thing is another, different thing. Some examples:

> The moon was a goblet of golden fire.
> The assassin's eyes were two poison balloons.
> The man was a dog.

The problem with using metaphors is that the reader might take your words at face value and think that the assassin really has poison balloons in place of his eyes, or that the man is literally a dog. A way to avoid this confusion is to inform the reader that you're using a metaphor in a footnote, like this:

> Paul opened the door. The assassin stood there, grinning. His eyes were two poison balloons.[1] Paul screamed.

---

1. Metaphor!

121

Observe Italo Calvino's masterful use of metaphor in *Mr. Palomar*:

> This is the hour when Mr. Palomar, belated by nature, takes his evening swim. He enters the sea, moves away from the shore, and the sun's reflection becomes a shining sword in the water stretching from shore to him. Mr. Palomar swims in that sword or, more precisely, that sword remains always before him; at every stroke of his, it retreats, and never allows him to overtake it.

Calvino's clever trick here is employing the sword metaphor to make this otherwise mundane beach scene feel like a video game. People would rather play fun video games than read books, but we force ourselves to read so that we can feel cultured and intelligent. Why not reward the reader by giving them that same feeling of playing a video game while they read your story? One could imagine a *Mr. Palomar* adaptation for Xbox or the Nintendo Switch, where the player must guide the title character through the water, avoiding various obstacles, until he can overtake the shining sword and move on to the next level. Many classic novels would probably be improved upon if they were turned into video games. *Crime and Punishment* could be a sort of *Grand Theft Auto* experience. *The Brothers Karamazov* could be like *Super Mario Bros*. Did you know that video games are a $120 billion industry? That's way more than even the film industry. I got into the wrong business. Complete morons write for video games— could you imagine if someone with my literary abilities came up with a game? These gaming nerds would absolutely lose their minds.

122

A motif is when you use a recurring object or idea in your story. That object or idea is repeated throughout your story to create a certain mood or establish theme. Think of the ducks in J. D. Salinger's *The Catcher in the Rye*, which come up again and again, and so are likely symbolic of something important. If you're having trouble coming up with a good motif, you can use Salinger's ducks. There's no copyright on having ducks in your book.

You can also make use of motifs to patch over awkward plot problems. Let's say you're working on the climax, where the main character finally confronts the novel's antagonist. The antagonist, a devious assassin, is pointing a loaded gun at your main character. How will your protagonist escape this impossible situation? You've written them into a corner—they're unarmed, trapped, and out of options. And so, because you need the story to progress, you have a gun drop from the sky and land in your protagonist's hand. They shoot the antagonist and save the day. While your plot issue has been resolved, astute readers might find it a little too convenient that a gun just happened to fall from the sky, right into your protagonist's hand at the perfect moment. If, however, you go back and make guns falling from the sky a recurring thing—a *motif*—then it will feel natural and earned. You could even change the first line of the novel to something like: "It was the year that guns fell from the sky." And then explain how a police officer trained her pet bird to fetch her service weapon, but then the bird escaped and taught this little gun-fetching trick to other birds, and now birds all over the country are flying around, stealing people's guns. And because guns are so heavy and birds are usually pretty small and weak, they end up dropping the guns. So you can now write in all of these scenes where guns fall from the sky because birds drop them, and people are so used to it at this point that they can easily catch the guns before they hit the ground. The reader will probably wonder what all this is about. "I'm enjoying this book," they might say, "but what's with the birds dropping guns and people catching them?" Once they reach the climax, however, where the main character catches a gun and shoots the antagonist, the reader will appreciate the big payoff and feel stupid for ever doubting you.

123

Sometimes traditional storytelling takes a back seat in a work of fiction, and the author instead focuses in on philosophical concerns and conceptual analysis. Such a work is referred to as a "novel of ideas." Take a look at this excerpt from *The Passion According to G.H.* by Clarice Lispector:

> All this gave me the light tone of pre-climax of someone who knows that, if I get to the bottom of objects, something of those objects will be given to me and in turn given back to the objects. Maybe it was that tone of pre-climax that I saw in the smiling haunted photograph of a face whose word is an inexpressive silence, every picture of a person is a picture of Mona Lisa.

Some readers might find writing like this somewhat difficult or inaccessible, but I've never had that problem. Dense, philosophical, and abstract works are like children's picture books to me. I don't need authors to hold my hand and walk me step by step through every little plot development and make sure I'm following along perfectly. I could read (and perfectly comprehend) *The Passion According to G.H.* while running an obstacle course.

But I am not a typical reader, and so you may have trouble finding a publisher if you decide to write works in this style. That's not really a concern for writers like me, however—we're only interested in creating compelling art. My next book, once I finish the Molly novel, will likely be a novel of ideas. It probably won't sell as well, but at least will please the critics. C'est la vie!

124

Many literary scholars examine works of fiction through the lens of psychoanalysis. With a psychoanalytic reading, the object is essentially to psychoanalyze a character in the story, or even the author themselves. If you want to add meaning and depth to your work, you can purposefully sculpt your story so that a psychoanalytic reading will be rewarded. To do this, you need to read about Sigmund Freud's concepts (Wikipedia is fine) and then put the things he talks about in your work. The big one is the Oedipus complex. This is based on the character from Greek mythology, Oedipus, who unknowingly kills his father and sleeps with his mother. Freud says we all have an unconscious desire to kill our same-sex parent and sleep with our opposite-sex parent. Your story can be read as an Oedipal narrative if you show a male character, for example, resenting his father and getting inexplicably horny around his mother. I thought about inserting the Oedipus complex into my Molly novel, but it didn't work. I wrote a scene where my mother came to my apartment and chastised me for dating her friend Molly, who was going through a divorce, and I added in that my character started getting a huge erection.

It didn't feel right, though. First, when my mother came over and yelled at me in real life, I didn't get an erection. No offense to my mother, but I just don't find her attractive. Plus, people yelling at me is a big turn-off. Second, for the Oedipal dynamic to work, I would also have to have a latent desire to kill my father—but my father died when I was a child. I don't even remember him. So how would that work? Finally, I realized that I'm not writing a story about my relationship with my parents. I'm writing about my relationship with an older woman, and how I had to outsmart and defeat her repulsive husband in order to secure her love. And that's enough. Sometimes a novel doesn't need any psychoanalytic gimmickry to have depth.

Revision

125

Let's say you've been working hard on your novel, making steady progress while you follow along with this guide, and now you've finally reached the end of the story. Time to pop the champagne, you might be thinking. You did it—you wrote an entire novel! Well, not so fast. I have some sobering news for you: finishing a first draft of a novel is only the beginning. Now the real work starts. Now it's time to edit.

The revision process can be gruelling, but it can also be incredibly rewarding. The beautiful thing about writing fiction is that you can go back, change things around, and spend as much time as you need to make everything perfect. In life, we're stuck with the choices we've made forever. I previously mentioned how, when we were still dating, Molly slipped on some ice and ended up in the hospital. She had a herniated disk and broke both of her arms. She had to have a couple of very minor operations and spent twelve days at St. Joseph's. And during that time—almost two full weeks—I did not visit her once. When she called, I said I was too busy with my writing, that I was filled with creative energy. I needed to take advantage of this inspired state by focusing all of my attention on my novel until the energy inevitably dissipated. The doctors had everything under control, I argued. What could I do? But truthfully, I was not especially inspired at the time. I did pick away at my novel, yes, but I spent most of that period watching television. I remember I binge-watched seasons fifteen through eighteen of *Family Guy*. The real reason I didn't visit Molly in the hospital was that I didn't want to see her sisters and her friends. They would interrogate me, judge me. Watch how I acted around her. Question me about everything. Molly's ex-husband Charles would likely stop by, too, I knew. He thought I was a dog catcher. I was also nervous about seeing Molly laid up in that hospital bed without makeup, her hair matted on the pillow, her skin all grey and loose. The whole thing filled my mind with dread, and so I decided to steer clear. Perhaps it was time for a change, I thought. I can't look after this sickly old woman. Why should that be my responsibility? This whole experiment had gone too far. Maybe we needed to call it a day. My mother phoned repeatedly, but I didn't answer. She eventually came by the apartment and Herman let her in. She scolded me like I was a child, told me how upset Molly was that I wouldn't visit. "I thought you didn't even want me to date Molly," I said. My mom just shook her head and left.

When Molly finally left the hospital, I did eventually go over to her apartment and see her. I brought her chicken noodle soup from the grocery store deli but ended up spilling it all over my pants before I got there. Things were a bit awkward between us. She said she wasn't mad at me for not coming to the hospital, and I said that that was good, she shouldn't be mad. I said I got a lot of important work done and that the doctors had everything under control. I said she ought to be more careful around icy sidewalks, especially at her age. I said I can't put my life and career on hold because of your carelessness. Then I told her about the soup I'd tried to bring her. I didn't stay long.

If only life was like writing fiction, and I could go back and revise things. Edit out all of the shameful choices I'd made. In this new draft, I'd be at Molly's bedside straight away. I'd stay there all week and sleep in a chair, if the nurses let me. I'd read to Molly from her favourite books, like *The Emerald*. I'd bring her chicken noodle soup every day and if I spilled it on my pants, I'd go back to the deli and order more. But life isn't like writing fiction. You can't go back and change things. You have to come to terms with the fact that things are bad now.

126

A story is only complete after it has gone through several drafts. With each of these drafts, you need to focus on a different aspect of the work. Think of it like judging a women's swimsuit competition: you can't assign scores based solely on the contestant's chest region. You need to look at their bum region too. A successful novel will similarly need to excel in a variety of categories. In this chapter, I will explain what elements you should be concentrating on with each draft, until you have a complete, polished manuscript.

127

With a first draft, your only concern should be to fill up the pages. Let your creativity flow freely. Don't worry about the plot coming together perfectly or having fully fleshed-out characters at this point. You don't even need to spell things correctly. You will fix all of this stuff in subsequent drafts—for now, just write down *some*thing. If you find yourself stuck, take an earlier chapter and paste it in again later. Borrow a few chapters from someone else's novel. Why not? You'll be revising all of this anyway. Right now, the goal is to simply to fill up a document with 40,000 words, which is the minimum length of a novel according to Wikipedia. If half of those words are your first chapter copied and pasted eight times, and the other half is a long excerpt from *Giovanni's Room*, that's all fine. You'll spruce things up as you move through the revision process.

128

The second draft is all about names. When composing a first draft, I name all of my characters Paul, so that I don't have to slow down and think up interesting names for everyone. Now it's time to sort through all of the Pauls and give them each their own unique name, so the reader doesn't become confused. One character can still be called Paul—your protagonist, preferably, because their name will come up most frequently and so you won't have to make as many edits. And now that all of your characters have their own names, it will be easier for you to tell them apart as you continue on with your revisions. You can come up with last names for the characters too, if you want, but I'd honestly worry about that in another draft.

129

For the third draft, run a quick spell-check. Your word processing software should have a spell-check feature that will do this for you. One thing to watch out for: if you spell a word wrong, but that misspelled word is actually a different, correctly spelled word, the spell-check won't pick this up. For example, you might accidentally type "bard" instead of "bird." A bard is an actual thing: it means an old-timey storyteller guy, and so spell-check will think that you meant to type "bard." Because of this, your story might include something like "The yellow bard flew in through the window." This is obviously ridiculous, because it would mean that a yellow storyteller guy flew in through the window. There's nothing you can really do about this problem, until we see an advancement in spell-check technology. Hopefully you'll catch these little errors at some point. They can, however, lead to happy accidents. Maybe a story about a yellow storyteller that flies around could be pretty interesting. In fact, that definitely sounds more compelling than some boring story about a yellow bird.

130

It can be helpful to look over your work while in an altered state of mind, because you will see things from a new perspective. Smoke a joint, drop acid, or chug a bottle of wine and then dive in. Personally, I'm scared of most drugs, so I just drink wine for this draft. One time, I smoked a little bit of weed and I couldn't stop thinking about killing myself. Wine is good though. The dulling effect of alcohol temporarily lowers your intellect, which can give you insight into how the average reader will experience your book. If you're scared of drugs like me and you're a teetotaler, there are other options. You can place your forehead on the end of a baseball bat and then run around in circles until you're dizzy. The effect doesn't last long though, so you'll have to keep doing it. You could also try and stay awake for three straight days, which makes you hallucinate. I've heard this can cause permanent brain damage, though. Maybe stay awake for two days, instead of three. You won't hallucinate, but you'll be really tired and that's definitely a kind of altered state.

131

We all have an inner, protective voice that tries to shield us from criticism. This voice can hinder a writer's ability to edit. For instance, you might be reading through a story you're working on and come across a sentence that feels slightly awkward. You puzzle over how to fix the sentence for a few minutes, when the voice chimes in: "Oh, it's perfectly fine. Don't worry about it. Move on." Or maybe you realize your protagonist does something completely out of character. Imagine it's been established that this protagonist is lactose intolerant, and you find a scene where they chug a gallon of milk. "Just leave it," the protective voice then whispers. "Nobody keeps track of stuff like that. It's only milk. It's not like they're drinking poison." And so the revisions suffer.

It's important to recognize and then ignore this voice. It will try to convince you that the problems in your story aren't problems, and this will prevent your work from improving. It's like when you're in a relationship with someone and things aren't working out the way you'd hoped they would. Issues between you and your romantic partner go unresolved because the voice tells you that everything is fine, even though everything isn't fine. Around the time Molly came home from the hospital after slipping on the ice, things between us had clearly soured. We weren't communicating the way we had been before. The fun and spontaneity of the early days of our courtship had vanished, with Molly lying around in bed all day recuperating. I'd thought our age difference would be negligible, but seeing Molly's frail body incapacitated highlighted how incompatible we really were. Molly didn't seem to notice all this, however. The little protective voice in her head was telling her that everything was fine. I knew things had turned for the worse, but I couldn't break things off. I'd been the one to convince her to officially leave her husband. Their reconciliation had been impossible because of me. Molly's sisters and friends already disapproved of me—I could only imagine the scorn they'd send my way if I were to now break up with Molly. I had to do something though. I needed to penetrate Molly's protective layer and silence the little voice holding her back from ending things. I needed to somehow convince her to break up with me. It was the only way.

And so, on subsequent visits to Molly's apartment, as she rested in bed, hopped up on pain medication, I laid the groundwork for my own dismissal. "It's clear that you're not interested in me anymore," I'd say. "Just get it over with already. Put me out of my misery." Of course, Molly would protest and try to reassure me. "No, no," I'd say. "Don't try and hide it. You don't care about me anymore. I can tell because you actually did care about me before, so I know what that felt like. I see where this is heading." It took a few weeks, but my tactics eventually paid off.

I was over at Molly's one evening, accusing her of not being in love with me, when she let out a long sigh. "This isn't working," she said. "I knew it," I said. I grabbed my jacket and got out of there in a matter of seconds. It was over. I was free. Molly had finally silenced her inner, protective voice and edited me out of her manuscript.

If only I had realized what that really meant. If I could have known the amount of pain that was coming my way. Oh, Molly.

132

Your next step should be the lay down/lie down/laid down draft.
I've been trying to think of a better name for this one, but it's
impossible. Anyway, the lay down/lie down/laid down draft is
where you go through and find all of the moments where characters lay down or lie down, or they lay objects down, and so on.
The grammar in these moments is overly complicated: does Paul
lie down in the bed, or lay down in it? Did Paul lay down his sword
on the battlefield, or did he laid it down? Or lie it down? Writers
drive themselves crazy trying to sort all of this out. Just have
characters jump into bed, or flop into bed, or onto the grass or
whatever. And then have them *put* their swords down. You could
even let the characters hold on to their swords indefinitely—it is
a story after all. Swords are exciting for the reader. If anything,
your characters should be picking up more swords, not laying/
lying down the ones they already have.

133

The next draft is all about cutting. Don't be precious with your writing—a story will always benefit when extraneous words are omitted. You want to try and pare the manuscript down to what's essential. If everything in your story seems indispensable, then cut randomly. Two or three sentences per page should be removed at minimum. Every tenth paragraph needs to go. Hell, cut everything. Start over. Why not? Even if the thing you were working on was going really well, you'll have learned from that experience and so what you write next will inevitably be better. I can't count how many times I've abandoned a project I'd spent months working on, because I knew the next project would be superior. And then a few months later, I'd start over again. Don't place everything you write on a pedestal. Keep writing and throwing everything away until you finally have something that's actually worth a damn. And then throw *that* away. The next one will be even better.

134

Many writers—myself included—spend most of their time writing in one spot. For me, it's at the little desk in the corner of my bedroom. Whether you write in your bedroom, a separate home office, a café, or a boxcar rattling through the American Midwest, it can be helpful to read through your work and make notes in an alternative location. This change of scenery will put you in a new headspace, and allow you to view your manuscript with a fresh perspective. I used to always bring my stories to work at Value Village once I reached this stage in my revisions, and set up shop in the employee bathroom. I'd sit on the toilet, hold the manuscript print-out in my lap, and when I finished reading through and marking up a page, I'd place it on the side of the sink. I'd prop my notebook up on top of the toilet paper dispenser, in case I needed to make more general notes. I usually kept a little snack in my breast pocket, like sunflower seeds, and my Sprite or water bottle sat on the floor by my feet. The motorized fan was quite loud and blocked out any store noise that might have otherwise distracted me. It was a pretty good setup. I was able to look over my work in this new physical space, which always gave me fresh insights, and it also allowed me respite from the never-ending line-ups at cash. I had to lie to my supervisors and say that I had severe irritable bowel syndrome to excuse these frequent and extended bathroom breaks, which was pretty embarrassing. Sometimes I'd spend the majority of my shift in there, editing prose and eating snacks. Other employees would knock on the door, and I'd let out pained groans in response. This little makeshift office made going to work more bearable, however, and I was able to use my work time productively, instead of wasting it helping customers. Plus, technically, I was getting paid to write, which is becoming increasingly rare in this business. Unfortunately, I was recently let go from Value Village and so I no longer have access to the employee bathroom. Firing someone for having severe irritable bowel syndrome is discrimination and I would definitely sue the company for all it's worth, if it wasn't for the fact that I don't actually have irritable bowel syndrome. But they don't know that. They claimed they were firing me for stealing books and clothes, except that doesn't make any sense because everyone on staff takes things. They just *happened* to crack down on the guy with severe irritable bowel syndrome, sure.

135

The focus of your next draft should be to look for logical inconsistencies. Basically, make sure that everything that happens in your book makes sense. Every effect should have a reasonable cause, and every detail should be consistent within the world of your story. I once wrote a story that took place during the American Civil War, and only after submitting it to *The New Yorker* did I realize the protagonist's electric toothbrush was an anachronism. There were no electric toothbrushes back then, but I needed my main character to have one for the climactic scene where he's hiding in a cornfield from Confederate soldiers and his toothbrush accidentally turns on, giving away his location. When I resubmitted the story to *The New Yorker*, I fixed the issue by introducing a new character—an eccentric scientist who invents the electric toothbrush and gifts it to his best friend, the protagonist of the story, on his birthday. The new character ended up being so compelling, however, that I cut out the Civil War elements and focused in on this crazy inventor messing around in his lab and getting into funny predicaments. *The New Yorker* passed again, but I may resubmit it as a cartoon.

136

Readers need to buy into the world of your story. If they become skeptical of your character's choices, or whether an event would reasonably take place in the fictional universe you've created, they will lose interest and stop reading. And the fact that something actually happened to you in real life doesn't guarantee that readers will find it believable in your novel. For instance, my uncle Herman recently kicked me out of his apartment and I had to move in with my mother. Herman said I was too messy, too inconsiderate, that I played the television in my room too loud, that I was always moaning and crying late at night, and that I never paid my share of the rent on time. All dubious accusations, easily contested. But what could I do? It was his place, and so I packed up my things and left. If you've been paying attention, however, you'll remember that my uncle Herman is mentally ill. He's legitimately insane, and gets himself into all sorts of crazy situations every day. So shouldn't I be the one kicking him out? Doesn't it make more sense that he's the one who is hard to live with, and I'm actually the normal one? It just doesn't feel believable that *he* would kick *me* out. If I were to try and include this occurrence in one of my stories, the reader would never buy it—even though that's what really happened.

Living with my mother isn't so bad, though. She brings me tea and little snacks while I'm writing. And now that I've lost my job, it's nice not to have to pay rent. It's funny how things kind of work out. I wonder what it would have been like if Molly and I never broke up, though. Because now I'm living in the building next to hers. I can picture it perfectly: I'm working at my desk and I get a call from Molly. I nip over for a quickie in her bed, then get right back to work on the novel. Eat some lunch, nip back over to Molly's. Another quickie. Nip home, see what Mother's up to. Or whatever. God, it would've been so convenient.

137

The focus of your next draft should be unity. Does everything in your story fit together as one piece? Do any sections feel out of place, or like a dramatic shift in tone occurs at any point? To illustrate, early on in the process of writing *The Emerald*, I was interested in classic horror fiction. As I read through H. P. Lovecraft and Shirley Jackson stories, elements of horror began showing up in my own novel. Later on in the process, however, I lost interest in the genre and began to read more comedic works. I became obsessed with watching *Saturday Night Live*, too, and this started to influence my writing. *The Emerald* became more of a satire piece. This meant that my novel ended up suffering from a lack of unity: what started out as an unsettling, macabre affair suddenly switched over to a madcap comedic romp. To fix this, I went back to the earlier passages and changed all of the grotesque, ominous characters into funny Walmart greeters and bellboys who run around their hotels all stressed out. The mysterious scraping sounds that the protagonist hears from their bedroom at night became the upstairs neighbour queefing. In the original draft, the main character opened his front door one night to find an enormous Cthulhu-inspired creature standing there, with tentacles on its face and sharp scales and claws. I changed this creature into a man from an unspecified country who struggles with his English. "I come inside?" the man says. "My name-a Dildo. Need help with find job." And now, with these comical revisions in place, *The Emerald* feels much more balanced.

138

Now it's time to comb through your manuscript and get rid of any racist lines. No matter who you are or what your background is, little slurs or insensitive turns of phrases will always make their way into your stories somehow. I'm probably the least racist person you'll ever meet, and I always find incredibly racist material in early drafts of my work. You want to make sure that all of that's gone. That's just one of the ways in which us writers can fight against racial discrimination.

139

If you're writing a contemporary story, it should be noted that the publishing world moves at a glacial pace. By the time your story finally reaches readers, years will have passed. For that reason, it's important to go through and update all of your references so that they're as current with the times as possible once audiences actually encounter your work. I once wrote a noir-inspired story that leaned heavily into the vaping craze that seemed to be dominating the culture at the time. In classic noir fiction, cigarette smoking is ubiquitous, and I thought it might contemporize my story to replace this habit with more modern and fashionable e-cigarettes. Unfortunately, looking back on the story now, my hard-boiled detective character and his constant vaping feels a little dated. Vaping just didn't become normalized in the way I thought it would. Here's a short scene from the story, to give you an idea:

> I sat on the stack of wooden pallets, eyeing the empty lot for Vinnie's coupe. The waterfront was quiet, still. Just after midnight. A heavy fog had rolled in earlier. I had front row seats to watch the deal go down, invisible amongst the shadows and the crawling mist.

The minutes ticked by, then the hours. Vinnie and his goons were late. I burned through an entire 15 mil. bottle of Peppermint Squeeze. I refilled my vape's tank with Coconut Cream Pie and adjusted the voltage. I waited. I was seconds away from throwing in the towel when a pair of headlights faded in to view.

Vinnie. The car made a slow, cautious approach. In the harbour, a small fishing boat flashed its lights three times. I'd pegged it earlier—this would be the blackmailer.

And then I realized: the fog had broken up. If anyone happened to look over at the stack of pallets, they'd see me there. I needed to hide, and fast.

I was about to jump down, when my hand brushed my pants pocket. I felt a long, slender bulge—my e-cig. I could stay right where I was. I cracked my knuckles. I knew what I had to do.

140

Now it's time to focus on character motivation. Every character in your story needs to have behaviour that's consistent with their established personality. There needs to be a reason behind every action they take, and those reasons need to make sense for the character. Otherwise, the reader will smell bullshit. For this draft, read through the manuscript carefully, scrutinizing your characters to make sure they are always properly motivated to behave the way they do in your story. I had to deal with this exact issue in my Molly novel. Near the end of the book, my character wanted out of the relationship, but Molly's character wouldn't let go. My character had to trick Molly's character into breaking up with him. And while this actually happened in real life, it didn't feel real when transposed to a fictional form. Why would I want to ruin one of the best things that had ever happened to me? And why the hell would Molly fight so hard to save one of the worst things that had happened to her? Our motivations didn't make any sense. Even after Molly ended things, she kept calling, trying to patch things up. She apologized profusely, and even begged me to get back together with her. I acted like she had wounded me too deeply, that I couldn't forgive her for breaking my heart. I stopped answering my phone and, eventually, Molly stopped calling. Now that she's come to her senses and realizes it's in her best interests to stay away from me, the universe is balanced again. Molly's motivations now make sense. Mine too: I desperately want Molly back in my life. *Of course* I do. But just because a character or a person wants something, doesn't mean they can have it. Therein lies the core of human suffering.

141

You're almost there. It's time for the final draft. This last effort is often called a "cop draft." A cop draft is when you get a police officer to read your manuscript and provide feedback. They can tell you if your cop characters and depictions of police procedures are realistic. If your novel doesn't have any cop characters, the officer's feedback can still be helpful. Cops can notice things that aren't cop-related. It's not like all they think about is being a cop.

Once you listen to the officer's suggestions and incorporate the ones you find useful, you're done. You now have a completed manuscript. Take a moment to let this accomplishment sink in. But don't take too long—your biggest battle yet awaits. There's only one thing standing between you and your goal of becoming a successful writer, but it's a real doozy. It's time to take on the publishing industry.

The Biz

142

You might think that your first step toward publishing would be to procure a literary agent, but I would advise caution here. While agents can help place your manuscript on an editor's desk for consideration, their fees are often quite high. And, as with anything in life, the pricier an agent's services are, the more you'll get out of the relationship. The "free" agents, who don't charge their clients anything up front, all seem to ignore my emails—the sure sign of a shoddy, substandard operation. I decided to go all in and sign with the most expensive literary agent I could find online. The initial cost would surely pay for itself once the agent inevitably found me a lucrative book deal, I figured. I took out a small bank loan, borrowed the rest from my mother, and sent this agent—we'll call him Lester—the required reading and administrative fees. As soon as the cheque cleared, Lester stopped replying to my emails. I sent a follow-up letter through regular mail, as well, but there was no response. I'm sure there's a reasonable explanation for this, like perhaps Lester had some sort of accident. Part of me wonders, however, if I was scammed. It was odd that Lester's online ad said he was based in

Manhattan, but I had to send my cheque to the Philippines. I'm sure I'm just being paranoid, though, and I'll hear from Lester soon. He's likely busy shopping *The Emerald* around and doesn't want to bother me until he has good news to deliver.

143

There are two traditional avenues for publishing fiction: large publishing companies, like Penguin Random House, and small literary presses, like Coffee House Press. There are benefits and drawbacks that come with each style of publisher. Large presses are only concerned with marketability and base their acquisitions on what has sold well in the past. Because of this, the big companies rarely publish anything interesting. Small presses, however, are where writers send their work after it's been rejected by the large presses. Due to this fact, small presses receive second-rate submissions. They have to choose their titles from a pile of rejected books. The sad truth is that neither large nor small presses publish anything of literary value anymore. The books truly worth reading, which contribute to the cultural advancement of society, only exist as .doc files on their author's laptops. That being said, you want to at least try and get your work published if you want people to read it. I'd go for the big publishers first, because they pay more, and then you can settle for a small press if they pass. If the small presses reject your manuscript as well, don't feel discouraged. None of these publishers would give James

Joyce's *Ulysses* a passing glance if it was sent to them today. What a crazy book, they'd say. We can't sell that. They'd probably turn their noses up at *Pride and Prejudice*. Too old-fashioned. They even reject *my* books. You're in good company.

144

Rejection is an important part of the writing process. You are going to encounter rejection over and over again, so it's important to grow a thick skin. Remember that you're not alone: just about every author encounters some degree of rejection throughout their career, especially early on. When John le Carré submitted his first novel, *The Spy Who Came in From the Cold*, one publisher wrote his agent, "You're welcome to le Carré—he hasn't got any future." That novel was eventually published and became an international bestseller. Joseph Heller's comic classic *Catch-22* was apparently named after the twenty-two rejections his manuscript received. One editor responded to Louisa May Alcott's submission of *Little Women* by suggesting that the author "stick to teaching." There are endless examples just like this.

If you're still feeling down about seeing your work rejected, consider what happened to the French writer Albert Camus. He died in a car accident at age forty-six. He was returning home from a vacation with his publisher, Michel Gallimard, when Gallimard's Facel Vega HK500 crashed into a tree on Route nationale 5. Camus wasn't wearing his seat belt and died instantly.

Gallimard died in the hospital a few days later. Imagine being in Gallimard's shoes: you kill your friend, spend a few days agonizing over this fact, while in horrible pain yourself, and then you also die. I'll take a few lousy manuscript rejections over that nightmare any day.

And then there's the Kali River goonch attacks. The Kali River goonch attacks took place along the Kali River in India and Nepal, between 1998 and 2007. In three separate incidents, young men were pulled under by a mysterious force while swimming in the Kali. The bodies of these boys were never recovered. It's suspected that they were dragged under and consumed by a 200 pound man-eating catfish called the goonch. The goonches in this specific section of the Kali River had grown to such a massive size and developed a taste for human flesh because they'd been eating the burnt human remains from funeral pyres that had been discarded into the water. Imagine enjoying a nice afternoon swim, and a 200 pound goonch grabs hold of one of your legs and pulls you down. Then the goonch just consumes you, bite after bite, like it's chomping down on a bread stick. This crazy, ravenous goonch that's addicted to eating partially burnt human corpses. Look up pictures of these giant Kali River goonches when you have a second. While a great white shark has the menacing appearance of a cold-blooded assassin, a goonch looks like a big log of shit, which is somehow more frightening. After I learned about the goonch attacks, I didn't sleep for a week. I certainly stopped caring about manuscript rejections. I'd give up writing forever if it meant I never had to encounter one of these goonches.

145

When I first started receiving rejections for my work, early in my writing career, I was always furious. I would respond to each one with incredulity: "How dare you, sir," I wrote to one editor. "You *will* regret passing up this opportunity. You *will* look like an absolute fool, come awards season. I guarantee it." I couldn't understand why these publishers weren't recognizing my brilliance. "You're discriminating against me because I don't have an aunt or cousin who works for you," I wrote another editor. "I smell nepotism." I even threatened a few publishers with legal action, but they could probably tell that I was bluffing. As I matured, however, I learned to brush the steady stream of no's aside. You have to embrace rejection as part of the process. When an editor says they're passing on your book, don't try and intimidate them into changing their mind with a menacing handwritten note or series of ominous, whispered voice mails—this never ends up working. Take the loss and focus on your next submission.

I'm still learning how to accept the hard truths life sometimes serves up. I just returned from Molly's ex-husband's house, where

I encountered a rather unpleasant scene. I went there so I could deliver an apology letter to Charles:

> I'm sorry for standing in your way. Molly deserves to be with someone who treats her right, and I now believe that that someone is you. Hopefully she realizes this, too. You have my blessing to pursue a relationship with Molly.

I signed the note "a friend." Before dropping it in Charles's mailbox, I noticed that the lights were on inside the house and I decided to peek through his living room window. One last look at my nemesis, before I conceded victory. I got up on my toes in Charles's garden and peered through the crack in his blinds. There she was—I nearly screamed but caught myself. My Molly. She and Charles sitting together on the couch. Two glasses of wine on the coffee table. They were smiling, laughing. A hand on her shoulder. She wasn't batting it away.

I couldn't believe it. I almost screamed again. Instead, I ripped out two fistfuls of flowers from the garden I was standing in. I went around to the front of the house and crept up next to Charles's car. I opened the gas cap and crammed the flowers inside. The note I'd written, too. Then I ran off.

When I returned home, Mother could tell I was upset. She sat me down in the kitchen and brewed me a cup of tea. She asked what was wrong and I said I didn't want to talk about it. We just sat there together, silently sipping our teas. I eventually calmed down. I went to bed but lay awake for hours, thinking about what I'd seen through Charles's window. There was no reason to be mad. What I'd written in the now gas-soaked note was true: Molly deserved to be with Charles. This was a good thing. Not for me, perhaps, but good for the universe. I accepted this. It was time to move on.

146

A note about pen names: writers may adopt a *nom de plume* in order to affect a new personality, signal that a work is stylistically separate from the author's other publications, or remain anonymous for personal reasons. When deciding on a pen name, you want to come up with something distinct and memorable—one that will stand out on a book spine amidst the other names populating a shelf. I have created a list of strong pseudonyms for you to choose from, if you're having trouble thinking of one on your own. If you see a name that you like, I would do a quick Google search first, to make sure another reader of this guide hasn't achieved literary success with it already. And if *you* are the one to achieve literary success with one of these pen names, please be courteous and include my name and website in your book's acknowledgements. Here are the names, presented in the order in which I thought of them:

Smoud Leemod

Tone Pasmin

Verdo Hobar

Sutton Minder

Werm Hermini

Cayman Gates

Rib Sanders

Fossel Cornet

Peef Doobin

Tino Emosh

Ainsy Trebido

Nubbins Horby

Wolfer Peets

Goth Bumers

Dade McTeenin

Big Nasters

Ogbert Bastille

Purb Windee

Flute Snats

Geef Malandis

Bobina Crim

Bolf Porkfat

Backfat Stumpers

Fatty Bigwind

Chunky Bigrolls

Gutfuck Windass

Chubs Buttrub

Paunch Jellyroll

Rolls "Backfat" Redbelly

Porky Hosedown

147

When approaching an editor, you want to compare your manuscript to the books the publisher has had the most success with, in terms of sales. If it's a smaller press, they likely haven't had any bestsellers, so you can compare your work to books they *wish* they sold. The bestselling book of all time is the Bible, but you don't want to come across as too churchy. The Harry Potter books have enormous sales, but publishers will think you've written a children's book and that market's over-saturated. To be honest, you're better off comparing your book to a movie. Hardly anyone reads fiction anymore, but everyone watches movies. The highest grossing films are all action-oriented Marvel and Star Wars affairs, which won't easily translate into a literary pitch. You want to go with popular movies that intelligent people enjoy. Academy Award stuff. *The English Patient* won Best Picture, for example. *One Flew Over the Cuckoo's Nest. The Godfather.* You could even write something like "What if *The Godfather* was a book?" Or "Imagine reading *The English Patient*, instead of watching it—that's my novel."

148

Many authors submit short stories to literary journals. This can help new writers get their names out there and gain experience working with editors. The problem with literary journals is that nobody reads them. If your story appears in *The New Yorker*, yes, people will pay attention. But good luck with that. I've been submitting to *The New Yorker* for over a decade, and my stories are actually good. The literary journals that might agree to publish your stories only exist as pet projects for bored English professors with access to grant money. They have no idea what they're doing. One small journal, which shall remain nameless, had the audacity to reject a story of mine that had received the good rejection form letter from *The New Yorker*. So yes, the editors at *The New Yorker* thought my story was fantastic but just couldn't find a place for it in the issue, but some lame quarterly from the goddamn Prairies thought it wasn't up to snuff. Sure. Can you imagine someone actually purchasing and reading through the stories in a literary journal? Seems like a red flag to me. There's definitely something a little off about a person like that.

149

In crafting a submission letter for your novel, remember that sometimes less is more. You want to build an air of mystery around your book, so that the editor will be curious to read it. Here's the new submission letter I drafted for *The Emerald*:

Dear _____,

Will *The Emerald* finally reveal itself? Time will tell...

Sincerely,
Sam Shelstad, Professional Author.

150

In all of your correspondence with editors and agents, be sure
to attach a professional photo of yourself. This will put a face
to your name and humanize you, which might prevent a hasty
rejection. For the photo, don't look right at the camera. Look
slightly up and off to the side, as if contemplating something.
This will show that you are a thoughtful, thinking person. Stand
in front of someone's parked sports car or elaborate water feature, giving the impression that you are wealthy—people will
want to be associated with your success. Wear a suit jacket over
a faded band T-shirt, showing your range. Hold a metal lunch
pail, signalling your working-class credibility. Crocs on your feet
will indicate a certain pragmatism that will make publishers
want to work with you. Either brush your teeth, or keep your
mouth closed. A stylish hat can work wonders if you have weird
hair. If your look leans too heavily toward egghead territory,
wear sunglasses. If you give off too much of a jock vibe, go for
thick prescription eyeglasses. Otherwise stick with transitional
lenses. One hand in your pocket will lend the photo a nice,

casual feel—but be sure it doesn't look like you're playing around with your genitals under there. No one wants to publish some masturbating creep.

151

Networking is a crucial skill for writers to learn, if they want to see any success. These days, with social media, networking is quite simple. First, find and befriend other writers on Facebook and Twitter (or whatever platforms are relevant when you're reading this). Preferably, try and locate writers at the beginning of their careers; ones who have a book out with a small press, say, but haven't sold many copies. As long as they aren't someone terribly famous, like Salman Rushdie, they'll likely accept your friendship request or follow you back. Now you can message them directly. Introduce yourself as a fellow writer, briefly, and then tell them how much you adored their book. Really lay it on thick. You don't have to actually read their book—it's not like they're going to quiz you. As soon as they receive your message, these authors will now see you as an ally and you can ask them for favours down the line. "Your book is actually pretty similar to the one I'm working on," you might message one of your new writer friends, once they achieve some greater literary success. "It's like we have the same brain...I wonder if your publisher would want to read my novel? lol!"

152

Through the process of writing this guidebook and the Molly novel, I've been afforded a chance to reflect on things. This has helped me to recognize that I have built up a considerable amount of emotional baggage over the years. I need to step back and take the time to work on myself. I now see that I simply wasn't ready for Molly. Perhaps in a few years, Charles will die of a heart attack or rare bone disease, and Molly and I can pick things back up. But only if I've worked through my issues and I'm ready to be the kind of loving, supportive partner she deserves. And with Charles dead and buried, we won't have to deal with the awkwardness of him running around all sad in the background, souring things, like he did the first time Molly and I dated. Or, who knows, maybe Molly will expire first. I'll approach Charles at the funeral, and we'll shake hands. "You're the only other person in the universe who understands how I'm feeling," Charles will say. "To love and to be loved by Molly. God, she was a good woman. Wasn't she?" I'll simply nod, pat him on the back.

The other great realization to come out of all of this is that I need to take responsibility for my writing career. I can't sit around waiting for publishers to pull their heads out of their asses and take a chance on me. I need to rely on myself and my own hard work, not the whims of flaky editors. I've decided to self-publish *The Emerald*. It's a different world now—we don't need these finicky gatekeepers dictating who gets to share their art. I can put my books out myself and sell them directly to readers. It won't be hard to find an audience, because I have over six hundred Facebook friends. If all six hundred or so of these contacts buy my book, which is definitely possible, and then they convince *their* friends to buy it, and so on, I could have a bestseller on my hands within a few months. All without agents and editors and publicists running around, siphoning money from me, forcing me to compromise my literary craft for the sake of the marketplace. I've already found a site that will set me up with everything I need to self-publish. All I had to do was order their comprehensive starter kit, which I sent away for yesterday. The address was in the Philippines, which is crazy because that's where my agent receives his mail as well. Perhaps it's fate. But I'll be able to pay my mother back for the starter kit soon, once I begin selling *The Emerald*, and then who knows. Maybe I'll self-publish the Molly novel as well. It's funny that I've never thought of doing this before. I could start my own press, actually. Writers can send me *their* submissions. And I'll personally reply to every single one of them. Even if I don't want to publish their book, I'll write back. No writer left behind. Unless they send me sci-fi trash, or work that feels derivative or overly sentimental. I'm not engaging with historical fiction in any way, either—what a snooze. Or anything that feels too Canadian. You know the kind of books I'm talking about. Please don't waste my time.

153

As I've matured, I've come to realize that if just one reader is able to appreciate your stories and get something real out of them, all of the hard work you've put in will have been worth it. In light of this, I decided to print off my now-completed Molly manuscript and drop it off at Molly's place. While countless others will surely enjoy the novel once properly released, I want Molly to read it first. If I die in a sudden accident and the manuscript gets lost, at least she'll have experienced my final literary statement. And I know she'll appreciate it.

I pressed a number of random buzzers in Molly's lobby until someone let me in the front entrance, and then I took the elevator up and placed my manuscript on the ground in front of her door. Whenever she steps out to run an errand, I figured, she'll see it sitting there and smile. The plans she had in mind will collapse in an instant, and she'll rush back inside to begin reading. I was on my way out of the building, however, when I started to worry that a neighbour might swipe the manuscript. A fair amount of elderly people populate Molly's building, and elderly people like to steal things. Or a dog could pass by and take a big chomp. I hurried back up and sat in the corner of the hallway, next to the stairwell, to keep watch. Make sure Molly, and only Molly, received my gift. After a few hours, however, the building superintendent stepped off of the elevator and spotted me crouched in the corner. He ordered me off the premises. Hopefully *he* didn't take the manuscript. Superintendents are notorious thieves, too. They're worse than seniors. That's why they take on the superintendent job—so they can go into people's apartments whenever they want and take stuff. It's becoming a real problem, I hear. Sometimes I wonder if some of the more old-fashioned publishers I've submitted to have sent me enthusiastic offers through the mail, but their letters have been swiped by my building super. It's actually highly possible that this has happened to me, which is pretty disturbing to think about.

154

Last night, Uncle Herman came over to my mother's for dinner. It was awkward at first—I hadn't seen him since he kicked me out of the apartment. But we eventually settled into a nice groove, and it was actually kind of pleasant. The three of us, idly chatting away. I talked about the new book I'm working on. Mother had purchased one of the good chocolate cakes from Pusateri's. It was nice. I didn't think about Molly at all. I didn't think about Charles, or Ballast Books, or whether or not *The New Yorker* would accept my latest submission. None of that. Sometimes you can get so caught up in relationship drama and trying to get a book deal that you forget about the simple things.

In the end, the writing life isn't all about publishing. It's about the writing. And sitting down with the people you love and sharing a nice dinner. Shooting the breeze. Passing the potatoes. Stirring the gravy. Wiping the greasy mouth on the napkin.

Epilogue

About the Author

Sam Shelstad lives in Toronto. His debut novel, *Citizens of Light*, won the 2023 Crime Writers of Canada Award for Best First Crime Novel. He is the author of the short story collection *Cop House* and his fiction has appeared in magazines including *The Walrus* and *The New Quarterly*. He contributes to *McSweeney's Internet Tendency*. You can find him online at samshelstad.com.

At the very beginning of this book, I asked you to imagine a gymnasium filled with chests. Each chest contained either a deadly cobra or a story. There's a much larger locked chest in the centre of the room, as well, containing the world's greatest stories. The key to the big chest can be found inside the stomach of one of the cobras. The goal of this book, I stated, was to prepare you for the task of locating and killing all of the snakes until you found the key, so you could then access the good stories. You kill the snakes with writing techniques. Now, unless you simply skipped ahead to the epilogue for some reason, you should be able to do just that. You are a real writer of fiction, capable of bringing deep, impactful stories to life for your readers. I don't have anything to add to this idea but realized I should bring up the cobra/key metaphor again, since it has only been mentioned once and I titled the book after it.

Good luck out there, and happy writing.